MY DRAGON MASTER

Broken Souls 6

ALISA WOODS

Cover by BZN Studio

ISBN: 9798647922939

***My Dragon Master* (Broken Souls 6)**

I'm stuck in an endless loop...

The evil elves and their torture chair.

Or floating on a dark lake under a purple-gray sky.

One's a memory, and the other is a dream.

But no matter what I do, I can't break free.

I've always known the Universe was made of magic... but what if that magic is evil? What if there's no purpose, no kind and gentle Universe beckoning me, and the Tarot cards that have always faithfully guided me are a lie?

Maybe the card I've drawn is Death.

The elves have succeeded, my mind has shattered, and this is all that's left.

The Universe wasn't supposed to be this dark.

Daisy is trapped in a coma, traumatized by her torture at the hands of the Vardigah. Akkan has been waiting faithfully by her bedside, even though he's convinced the fates will conspire against them both. But if Daisy breaks the spell and awakens, the truth awaits discovery like a card before it's turned. And the Universe has more in store for them than either could possibly imagine...

My Dragon Master is a steamy dragon shifter romance that'll heat up the sheets with love and warm your heart with dragonfire.

ONE

Daisy

THEY'RE USING THEIR MAGIC WAND ON ME AGAIN.

Their energy is so cold. It radiates from them like Death, blowing across my skin… my mind… I'm trapped in their chair. They touch the crystal wand to my temple. *I scream.* So loud. It hurts my own ears, *my throat,* and my mind punches back against the assault, but it's my heart… my heart is tearing into pieces. I know Jayda hears me. She'll worry. And poor Grace—she's just a young one and so light of heart. This might break her.

It's breaking me.

I scream and scream, but the sound is far off now, fading like mist. The chair dissolves. The magic beings with their pointed ears blink away like they always do, leaving darkness behind. *This isn't real, Daisy.* It was real once, but this is just an echo. I know this, but its power is so strong, it holds me captive, like when they pinned me and tortured me. *But it's just a memory now,* I tell myself.

I survived.

The darkness lightens, and I'm floating again in an infinite lake of deep, calm waters. Above me is a troubled sky. Purple shimmers across graphite-gray clouds pregnant with rain. This is where I come to center myself. If I lie perfectly still, the clouds will keep their water above, and the darkness will stay down below. *Balance.* I can hold it, if I just breathe and live in the space between, floating between here and there. I've always been out of place. Not quite in the world, inhabiting the threshold between the earth of humanity and the magic of the Universe. It's always been abundantly clear to me, *visible,* this magic. In every life I've lived, it was there, just out of reach, whispering its secrets through the Tarot cards. I'd always thought—*hoped*—that someday, I'd breach the veil and touch the magical half of the Universe.

And then it came for me.

How horribly disappointing to find the magic was evil.

I ponder this as I float. The beings who tortured

me—I think they're elves. Their pointed ears are a sign, but they could be fae or pixies or even angels. Not that those creatures are real in the earthen realm, but then neither are elves. And the long, ugly faces? Their soulless eyes? It's like the stark coldness of their auras has frozen their bodies into a grimace. Then they pour all that malevolent energy into their crystal wand and use it to torment us— Jayda and Grace and me.

But for what purpose?

The water trembles around me. I sway, still floating at the surface while the darkness churns below and the purple-gray clouds convulse above. Each time I touch upon the *why* of all this, the balance threatens to upset. Then I get thrown back into that torture chair, triggering a flashback that's so real I can smell their alien bodies and feel the cold pinchers pressing into my legs through the folds of my skirt. Each time I'm drawn back there feels like it weakens me—it frays the tether that holds me, suspended between the realms.

What happens if it snaps?

I spread my hands on the water's surface and breathe, deep and slow. *Balance.*

I think of the Temperance card. It appears before me, massive, life-sized, hovering in the air as

I float above my troubles below. I've studied the cards for so long that I can see every detail, even though I'm conjuring this from memory, just like I did for all those readings back in the cells with Jayda and Grace. My deck at home is worn but top quality—I've carried it with me for years—and the artwork is gorgeous. Temperance is a young man with angel wings, the sun and the moon in each hand, a balance of forces, light and shadow, both material and spiritual. Temperance is strength. Patience. He would float in this placid lake for as long as it took to quell the passions below. Let the healing begin. I welcome the energy of this strong card. The Major Arcana are sources of power, and as I breathe it in, the image of Temperance dissolves into a mist that rains down on my face and body, granting me the positive energy I need.

I float a long time. Breathing.

Sometimes, I can stay here for days. Years? Time has no meaning in this realm. I know it is magic, just like the dark elves and their wand. I know the Universe has all manner of wonders yet to be revealed. But if I probe it too deeply—if I ask what all this is for—I'm quickly drawn back to the chair. It's like an endless loop, and I can't break free.

Haven't broken free. Yet. But if I have to be in this loop, better to be on the lake than in the chair.

I made promises to Jayda and Grace. That the Universe still had a purpose for them. That they had to survive because their purpose was unfulfilled. What of my purpose? I've always felt it was there, just out of reach as I was stumbling toward it. That eventually I would reach it.

What if it was all a lie?

The lake trembles beneath me.

I breathe in. Breathe out. The truth awaits discovery like a card before it's turned. What if the magic of the Universe is made of darkness? What if there's no purpose, no kind and gentle Universe beckoning us to our higher and greater selves? Maybe the card is Death, and that's all there is. Maybe Grace and Jayda have escaped or died. I could still be in the cells, the dark ones breaking my mind—or my soul, because I know that's what they're after. Maybe they've succeeded, and this is all that's left. Shattered pieces. The dark lake and the purple sky.

Is this forever?

Something stirs inside me, deep in my chest. That's a question, and a question is for the cards. I've read Tarot my entire life and several lifetimes before this one. Sometimes, I read for others, but mostly for myself. The cards don't foretell the future as much as guide you to your higher self, your purpose, bringing out the truths you already know.

I decide a simple draw is best. *Three cards.* Past, Present, and Future.

They appear above me, where Temperance was before, hovering, only these have yet to be turned. The star-burst pattern on the backs of the cards stares at me like unblinking eyes of cool-green radiance. I breathe deeply again, clearing my mind and readying myself to receive whatever message the cards will facilitate. I understand each one's symbology and significance, the many permutations and layers of meaning they can hold, but it's the connection with my own inner self that's most important. Given that my mind is conjuring these in the first place, it's doubly imperative that I open myself to whatever my fractured mind needs to tell me.

I briefly close my eyes, and when I open them, the first card is turned.

The Fool. Of course. This is my past. The girl in her full skirt and bare feet about to fall into a deep still lake. It's almost too close to where I am, and I wonder if I'm living in the card itself. I've always identified most with the Fool. The innocent knower of deeper truths. You can't live the many lives I have without bringing some of that with you. I always trusted in the greater goodness of the Universe, and maybe the cards are saying that trust was misplaced. It's part of my past, not my future.

I close my eyes again, a lengthy blink born of weariness. When I open them, the second card is turned.

The Chariot. This quickens my interest, bringing me more fully awake. The Chariot is drawn by two horses, one black, one white. It is definitely going somewhere, a young man crouched on the curtained car they pull, holding on for the ride. The Chariot signals that a choice is to be made, right now, here in the present. An action must be taken, but what? I don't even know the choices, but this card is dynamic, insistent. The moment is now.

I wet my lips and stare at the unturned third card. *The future.* Its promise is intrinsic. There will be a future. I'm not trapped here in the eternal present. Which has been hinted at by the Chariot. It's heralding the future and not very subtle about it, either. I pull in a breath, steady myself again on the surface of the lake, the Fool I am, and blink my eyes with a rather strident intention.

The third card turns.

The Emperor. I actually inhale with surprise. The Emperor is the divine masculine. *The Master.* He builds a better world, like the red desert planet he sits upon as his throne. The world, in turn, hovers above a cosmic chessboard. He's patient, wise, and calm, his gaze on the horizon. His legs are casually crossed, his arm resting on the back of the globe he rules. A king's chess piece dangles from his finger-tips. But there's something wrong about this card…

I squint, studying the Emperor's face. This isn't the card from my deck.

Then he moves.

It startles me so badly, I twitch in the water and almost lose my balance. I hold still again, my breath coming quick as my heart thuds in my chest.

The Emperor turns his far-away gaze to me. His eyes are slate-blue, beautiful and deep, and his face has the angular beauty of royalty. He's an Emperor of ancient Rome, pale-skinned and regal-nosed, but a face I've never seen. The corner of his mouth lifts into a soft and knowing smile as if he sees me seeing him, and it pleases him, this god among men. Tiny lines form at the corners of his eyes as the smile reaches them. A feeling of warmth spreads across my skin, like stepping into a sunspot during a walk in the woods. Everything relaxes. My lungs fill more easily. My shoulders loosen. Everything in this place seems suddenly new and sharp and wondrous, simply because he's here, seeing it.

And me.

His gaze relaxes my tired muscles, clenched too long, trying to keep the balance.

Still holding my gaze, he slowly uncrosses his legs and leans forward. *Out of the card.* His one hand still holds the king's chess piece, but the other extends down toward me.

He hovers above me, the hint of smile gone, the warmth faded from my skin, his hand waiting. The other two cards are motionless.

I know what the Chariot means now. I have to leave the Fool I've been and accept the Emperor's hand. Trust in his wise leadership. Believe that the Master knows the way back. *The way out.* Or stay forever in this place.

I want to lift my hand and take his, but this water I'm floating on is holding me. I'm wasted and frail, and lifting my arm out of the water feels like raising a thousand pounds by my fingertips. The lake trembles around me even with the thought.

But I'm determined. I focus. My hand shakes as I lift it infinitesimally from the surface. The water surges, making me sway. My arm smacks back down in the water then up again, the waves rocking me so much I can almost reach him.

The Emperor's hand stays fixed, waiting. I have to come to him. I have to *act*.

I strain and reach. The lake rumbles. The waves turn violent, tossing me so my arm swings, wild. Water soaks my skirt, my blouse, splashes my face. Even with great energy, great will, it seems like I'll never reach him. The gap is too much. The water is covering me now, each wave threatening to pull me down. I can't stay on the surface—can't keep the balance—if I want to have any chance of reaching him. I feel the scream building deep in my chest. The frustration and the determination. I let it build and then let it loose from my mouth, arching my back and lifting my hand to find his, but that only plunges my head back, into the water... I'm screaming under the waves, *drowning, drowning, drowning...*

His hand clasps mine and *pulls*.

TWO

Akkan

DAISY IS MY SLEEPING BEAUTY.

Her sleep is restless, filled with frowns and pursed lips and an occasional ominous word that whispers out. But her beauty is nearly restored. When our rescue team first arrived for her three weeks ago, I could scarcely believe she was alive. Cracked lips and sunken cheeks, the ghostly white of her skin, the utter stillness of her body... I thought we were too late. And, in the deepest, most honest place of my heart, I expected as much.

The fates have never been kind to me.

I've chased this spirit—Daisy's *dragon spirit*—for over two hundred years, never once reaching her. And now that I have, it's fitting the fates would deliver her body but keep her mind locked away inside. Her bruised and cracked lips have healed, but I fear her spirit may be forever broken.

Not *dead,* though. The Vardigah did *not* succeed in their quest to destroy her dragon spirit, that much I know. *I live...* so, therefore, her dragon must still be slumbering within her. Otherwise, I would have perished like Kashin, dropping dead suddenly, eyes wide in surprise as his other half was destroyed and his soul unexpectedly left his body. Not that I have much more time on this earth, either. There's only so long a dragon can last without mating, and I've lived longer than most.

If only I could awaken my sleeping beauty with a kiss.

Daisy sighs, a trembling sort of sound that verges on frustration.

I scoot to the edge of the plastic hospital chair, leaning in to hear any words that might escape from her lips... but she falls silent. My gaze is drawn for the millionth time to the machinery of the hospital. The steady trace of her heartbeat. The percent oxygen in her blood. All normal. The IV sustains her body with fluids and nutrients during the slumber from which she never truly wakes. When she first arrived at the hospital, here in the heart of New York City and not within the safe enclave of the North lair, I was vigilant—I feared the Vardigah might return for her. Then we discovered they'd been tracing the soul mates by the clothing and items they'd had in captivity. I quickly destroyed the bag of clothes leftover from Daisy's admission to Mount Sinai, so that danger was eliminated over a week ago. During her whole stay, I've brought the softest nightgowns I could find, creams for her skin when nurses' sponge baths left her raw, and a boar bristle brush for her beautiful blond hair. I've taken the liberty of brushing until it shines. The nurses have long ago stopped questioning my constant presence.

All because I don't want to miss the moment she'll finally come to me and open her eyes.

I don't even know their color.

Her fits of mumbled torment are the closest I've come to hearing her voice. I know almost nothing about this woman whose soul is my other half.

I think, perhaps, the fates are having their last good laugh at my expense. The final, cruel twist of the knife. At the same time, this feverish state is far better than the coma she's been in, as still as death. *Patience, Akkan.* You'd think I would have mastered that art by now. But I've been waiting two hundred and nine years for this woman, ever since I was a sixteen-year-old dragon going to meet a witch for his pairing. It didn't happen then, and every beat of my heart fears it will not happen now. Not even for a moment. At this point, I'd settle for just one. Just a chance to look her in the eyes and see if our connection really is any different than all those I've had with other women—all the ones I've known and bedded and even, on occasion, loved.

My soul mate. Did I really miss so much, all these years?

Daisy stirs again and then settles.

There's a soft knock at the hospital room door.

I rise quickly from my chair.

A beautiful black woman peeks in. "Okay if we come in?" she asks quietly. It's Jayda Williams, Daisy's friend from the time of their capture. I know her from the soul mates' files that Niko, Lord of the Lair, keeps—I've never met her in person, but I'm the one who asked her to come.

"Of course," I say in a natural speaking voice. If merely talking could wake Daisy, I would have been orating at full volume for as long as it took. I step around the bed, my hand extended as she swings the door more fully open. "I'm Akkan, Daisy's soul mate."

"Right." Her grip is firm. I clasp her hand with

both of mine.

Behind her, hovering at the door's threshold, is Grace Tanaka, another soul mate captured and tortured by the Vardigah.

"I didn't properly introduce myself the first time we met, Grace," I say.

She smiles, and it's much more radiant than the tortured one she had when she visited two weeks ago. "I was kind of a wreck."

"Not at all." I offer my hand to her as well—she's a little more tentative about the shake. She's mated now. Jayda as well. They both teleported here from their various love-nest retreats with their dragon mates, at my request. I feel the jealousy rumble deep within, but it's for my mate. These two weathered their trauma and, with the help of their mates, came back and are transformed. What have I done for mine but sit by her side and brush her hair?

I feel the pain of it deeper than even the jealousy can reach.

I step back to give them room. "Please come in."

As Jayda quietly closes the door, I drift back to Daisy's bedside. I've been here so long—three weeks, leaving only for meals and rest—that it almost feels unnatural not to be by her side. Her hands rest softly at her sides, but I'm so familiar with her rhythms, I can tell she's still in that restless not-sleeping, not-awake state. As if confirming, she pulls in a breath suddenly... and then slowly releases it.

Jayda frowns and moves closer to the head of the bed. "Oh, Daisy, where have you gone, girl?"

"Niko said she's been talking?" Grace grips the side rail of the bed, the one that keeps Daisy from slipping out should she move in her sleep. She rarely does.

"Just a whispered word, now and then," I say. "*'The shadow and the light. They're coming.'* Niko is convinced it means something, but I'm not so sure."

"Is she dreaming?" Jayda smooths back Daisy's hair, and Daisy seems to move in response to the touch. Jayda flicks a questioning look to me.

I shrug. "Nothing I've said or done has gotten a response from her. But she doesn't know me. I thought maybe you two—your voices, your presence—especially when she's in this fitful state, I was hoping that might make a difference. That the familiarity might reach her."

Jayda leans in, gently stroking Daisy's cheek. "Daisy, honey, it's Jayda. Gracie's here too. We're here for you, girl. And I know you're *strong*. Time for you to come back to us."

A long breathless moment stretches, but Daisy's even quieter than before.

"Do you know her last name?" I ask. "Or where she lives? I haven't been able to track down anything about her."

Grace looks distressed. "I can't believe we never asked what her last name was!"

Jayda pats her hand, which is still gripping the railing. "We had more pressing problems at the time." To me, she says, "I thought you dragons had your feelers out all over the world. Can't you track down one missing woman? Especially when she's not missing anymore?"

I sigh, frustrated by it as well. "She seems entirely off the radar. No image search or facial recognition searches bring up anything. Do you have any idea what she did for a living? Did she mention any relatives?"

Jayda and Grace exchange frowns.

Grace turns back to me. "She read Tarot all the time. Maybe she did readings?"

I give her a small smile. "That's something." There have to be ten thousand Tarot readers in New York. And there's no guarantee Daisy's from here. "You two lived in the city before you were taken, right? Do we know if Daisy was from here as well?"

Grace cringes. "God, we're the worst friends!"

Jayda chastises her with a look, then says to me, "I don't remember exactly her saying she was from the city, but I'm pretty sure she was." She frowns, thinking. "She didn't have an accent that I could discern."

"Like what?" Grace asks. "A New Yawker accent? No one has those anymore. I grew up here, and I don't."

Jayda lifts one eyebrow. "You have a *Rich Girl* accent, child."

"*Child?*" Grace pretends to be offended. "Is that Georgian for *Grace, you're a terrible friend?* Because I'm feeling that right now."

Jayda sighs and pulls Grace in for a one-armed hug. "You know what Daisy would say to that?"

"That I'm being melodramatic and should shut up?" Grace squishes up her nose.

"No, that's me." Jayda gives her a half-smile.

I smile too, but that pain deep in my chest wells up. What I'd give for Daisy to bounce back from her trauma like these two.

"Daisy would say we're doing the best we can,"

Jayda continues. "That the Universe has a plan for us or some shit. And then she'd be nicer than any normal human has a right to be. She'd be more worried about us than anything." Grace looks like she's tearing up. Jayda's one-armed hug tightens. "Don't you worry. She's going to get through this. You see how she's fighting? This girl has a dragon spirit if I've ever seen one."

I'm not sure which of us she's trying to convince. Grace just sniffs and nods.

"Hold up," Jayda says suddenly. She releases Grace and points a finger at me. "Daisy said something about needing to find a new place. The cat was possessed and had started throwing up in her shoes and how one shouldn't ignore signs from the Universe like that."

"She has a cat?" This surges alarm through me. Daisy was held captive for at least two weeks. It's been three weeks since we rescued her. I don't want her to wake only to find her beloved pet has starved to death...

"No, it wasn't hers," Grace says, brow furrowed. "It was her roommate's."

"I think she was couch surfing," Jayda explains. "I got the impression Daisy kind of floated around wherever the Universe sent her."

"That could explain why I can't find much on her." But it doesn't tamp down my alarm. Was Daisy homeless? The idea that my soul mate has been here in the city all along, suffering without my knowledge… the turmoil of that forces me to step back and pull in a breath. *There was nothing you could do, Akkan.* The reassurance is empty, though. My soul knows too well you can lose everything simply by not being where you were supposed to be.

Daisy moves, but in a different way from before —her whole body seems to stiffen.

I ease closer, and Jayda and Grace watch her as well. Her head twitches, a silent *no*, then the tension curls her shoulders forward, just slightly, but it's so strange, nothing like before, I'm afraid something's happening. I scan the monitor, and her heart rate has picked up. Blood pressure too. Nothing triggering any alarms, but still—

Daisy gasps—a sudden, massive intake of air —*and bolts straight up in the bed!*

I jolt and stumble back. Grace lets out a muffled cry.

"Oh, *shit!*" Jayda rears back, surprised.

Daisy's chest is heaving, her mouth gaped as she struggles to open her eyes…

Then she turns and looks straight at me. *"It's*

you," she whispers, her eyes finally going wide.

My heart lurches, but words are trapped in my frozen mind. Her eyes are beautiful—deep brown rimmed in black, dilated like she's been seeing a darkness for years. She blinks, several times, but never loses focus on me. *"I'm ready,"* she breathes, and I know she's speaking directly to me like she's waiting for some kind of order.

Only I have no idea what. My mouth just hangs open, my heart suspended. *She sees me.* Finally, after two hundred years, after three weeks in a coma, and *she's ready.*

And I'm standing before her completely speechless and unprepared.

A muffled sound draws Daisy's gaze—it's Grace, both hands over her mouth, her eyes glassed with tears. Jayda's expression is shocked joy.

"Oh, my *God!"* Grace gushes then lurches forward across the railing to throw her arms around Daisy.

It nearly knocks her over.

I'm there in a flash, my arm behind Daisy's back. *She's so frail.* It's like holding a bird in my hand and trying not to crush it. Her head rolls back, her eyes finding me again.

"Grace!" Jayda's chastising her and pulling her

back.

"*Shit.*" Grace practically curls in on herself.

But they both fade from my mind, my whole attention absorbed by Daisy's luminous eyes searching mine. "*I'm ready,*" she whispers again, but her body isn't. She's slumping, her eyes blinking rapidly, and I can barely lay her back before she's gone again, head falling to the side, breath escaping in one long sigh.

My heart's ready to explode. I turn to Jayda and Grace, the horror on their faces a mirror of my wordless torment. "Get the nurse," I finally manage to get out.

Jayda's eyes fly wide, and she whirls around, rushing out of the room.

"Oh, God. Oh, God." Grace covers her mouth with both hands.

My arm is still trapped under Daisy's once-more inert body. I slowly ease it out, my heart pounding as I scan the monitor. Her heartbeat is slow but steady. There's no reason to think she's any worse off than she was a minute ago. But the tightness in my chest says something different.

My sleeping beauty woke up. I had my one moment with my soul mate.

And I didn't say a thing.

THREE

Daisy

OPENING MY EYES IS GETTING EASIER.

The bone-deep weariness is lifting. Every time I wake up, I feel a little stronger. And I'm *sleeping* now. No more trembling lakes and purple clouds. No dreams at all. Just drifting off into a blissful nothingness, then waking up again, long enough to eat and use the facilities, and then I'm pretty wiped, and it's back to bed.

Each and every time, the Master is here.

I'm too tired to talk, and he asks nothing of me. Just holds my hand when I'm rising from the bed. Adjusts my pillow before I sink into it once again. Gives me privacy when the nurse comes for my sponge bath. I have to look like a drowned possum, but there's only kindness in his eyes.

I drift off each time, knowing he's waiting for me. Patient. Until I'm strong enough for whatever the Universe has sent him for.

I take a deep breath and stretch before I open my eyes. When I do, he's watching me. His slate-blue eyes are darker today, clouded by some unknown concern. He's an incredibly beautiful man, as an Emperor should be—sculpted cheeks above a precisely trimmed beard; long, loose hair that seems naturally decadent with a touch of wisdom; broad shoulders that carry his mandarin-collared shirt with a certain ease, the top buttons undone like a Greek prince in his afternoon casual attire.

"Good morning," he says with a smile, the same greeting no matter whether it's light or dark outside my hospital room window. "Your breakfast isn't too cold. Are you hungry?"

I nod because speaking is still rough.

He eases up from the chair in a fluid way that says he's comfortable in his body. I like to watch him move. It's like seeing a professional dancer walk across a room—we all do it, but not like they do. Their movement is art, made simply by pushing their bones and muscles through space. That's what the Master is—art in the form of a man.

I don't know his name yet. This space we're holding doesn't seem to require it.

He wheels back the tray that swings over my bed, then deftly removes the food tray coverings while I flail for the controls for the bed. He finds them before I do, and the mechanism whirs and lifts the head of it. I gaze at him while we wait. He has tiny lines at the corners of his eyes. They crinkle more when he sees me watching him. After a beat, the smile reaches his lips. Warmth spreads across my face, that same feeling as before, like stepping into a glorious sunspot in the middle of the forest. He was in his Tarot card form then, hovering over me and offering me passage back to the real world.

I can't help but wonder why.

"You look stronger this morning." He's pleased by this.

I glance at the window. The blue sky peeks through the slats. "Morning." My voice is still so gravelly. Every time I talk, it feels like sandpaper roughing up my throat.

"Yes." His voice is eager. He hands me the paper cup filled with juice.

I sip it down, soothing the ravages of my throat and drinking all I can. I set that next to the plate and contemplate the eggs and toast. No way I can manage the dry bread, so eggs, it is. My hands are steadier now, so I can feed myself. He still unwraps the fork from the plastic and hands it to me.

I don't want to complain, but I can do it myself. I make a show of taking a big stab at the eggs and chewing it, grandly. He seems amused, but then it's all too dry, and I need the juice again. I snag it off the tray before I can cough out eggs and make a mess, but my hand quivers on the way.

His expression clouds.

I choke down the egg-juice slurry and decide I need to make better choices in my life. Showing off for the Master isn't one of them.

When my mouth is clear, I take a breath and say, "I'm okay." I give him my most sincere look, so he'll know I mean it.

It works. The concern drops off his face. "Keep eating."

I obey, forking up the eggs at a more reasonable pace. I'm still working back to solid food anyway, so it's not like I can eat that much. I poke at a small cluster of grapes. As I'm contemplating those, he picks up the bunch, pulls one off, and pops it in his mouth. His wink is unexpected, as is the flush that runs through me.

I just stare, and his humor dissipates into something more solemn. He frowns as he returns the grapes to my tray. "Daisy, I…" He stops, seems to think for a moment, then meets my gaze. "You have to wonder why I'm here."

Ah. He's decided it's time. I want to say, *It's all right. I understand. The cards explained everything.* But that rarely goes well with people. Then again, the Master isn't an ordinary man. Any Fool could see that, and I'm the Queen of them.

I reach for the juice, swallow some down, then beckon him closer, so I don't have to speak loudly.

His eyes light up. His hands rest on the railing of the bed, and he leans on it to bend closer, turning his ear toward me while never letting his gaze fall from my face.

"You came for me," I rasp out.

He stays close, turning to look me in the eyes. "Yes. I did." He pierces my soul with that look. A strange mixture of the flush from before and the warm feeling of stepping into the sun seizes hold of my body. He lingers, close, like he's drinking me in and on the verge of spilling the secrets of the Universe—

Then he pulls back.

It's like being set loose from orbiting the sun. I'm unmoored, unanchored, but more… I'm simply exhausted. The intensity of that one, almost-wordless encounter with this magical man has drained what little reserves I have. I lean back on the raised head of the bed, my eyes falling closed just for a moment.

He says nothing.

I open my eyes even though I feel the pull of that deep, dreamless sleep of recovery. "I'm sorry," I whisper.

There's turmoil on his face, but it's more than my brain can decipher. He finds the bed controls, and a moment later, I'm sinking back down, the head lowering to the sleeping position.

By the time it reaches the bottom, I'm already drifting into darkness.

I don't know how long I've slept—I never do—but this time, when I awake, something's different. There's an energy level I haven't had before. My throat is less sore. I'm feeling human again. All of which feels like an amazing gift from the Universe until I realize...

The Master is gone.

My heart leaps. I scan my room, but there's

nowhere he could be hiding—it's a private room with just my bed and monitors, a TV and dresser I never use, the windows leaking sunshine again, and the tiny bathroom next to them. The door to the nurses' station is closed, and there's definitely no one in the room but me.

Did I scare him off? Or, more likely, I disappointed him. I just haven't recovered fast enough for whatever purpose he has for me. *I'm taking too long.* The adrenaline of that—*the Universe has finally come through with my purpose, and I've missed it!*—propels me out of bed. The linoleum floor is cold on my bare feet. My loose cotton nightgown swings around my knees as I hobble to the door with barely-awake legs. I fumble at the paddle doorknob—*is it ridiculously difficult to work or am I just weak?*—and I finally get it to turn. I shuffle back, swinging open the door—

He's there. Holding a coffee cup, one hand extended like he was reaching for the door. "You're up." He's startled. It's so different from his normal expression—calm and serious, wise with the strength of the Universe—that I just gape for a moment.

Then I'm so glad to see him, I bumble out, "You were gone." The last word catches, and I have to cough through it, but my throat feels almost normal again.

Pain washes across his face—it stuns me to see it —then he says, "I just stepped out for a moment." Like he's *apologizing*.

Which makes no sense at all. "No, I... it's my fault..." I step back to give him room to come in, but I'm feeling suddenly light-headed, so I clutch the edge of the door.

"There's literally nothing that's your fault, Daisy." The deep timbre of his voice settles me, like the sound of the ocean on a bright summer's day. He steps closer and offers his arm. I clutch that instead of the door. "No matter what else you might think, don't ever think you're to blame for any of this." The strength of his arm—it's like steel under the thin cotton of his tailored white shirt—is even more reassuring than his words. I know getting kidnapped by the dark elves wasn't my fault. I'm not the kind to take personal responsibility for the vagaries of the Universe. But I also know you have to do your part when it sends you an opportunity. I don't even know what opportunity the Master has to offer, but I know the Universe brought him.

"Don't give up on me," I say as we shuffle back toward my bed.

"I'm not. I never would." His words are a balm against my fears.

Before we reach the bed, the nurse comes bustling in behind us. "Oh, you're up, Miss Daisy!" she sings. She's a lovely Hispanic woman who seems unnaturally cheery all the time. Some people are just like that. The nurses cycle through like crazy, and I can't track them all, but this one's name is Lucía, and I love the sound of it, so it sticks in my scattered mind like taffy. "It's time for your shower, lady! Let's get you all cleaned up." She scurries around my other side, opposite the Master, and takes my arm. "We'll just be a little while," she says to him, but it's clear she's not taking no for an answer. And given I've had nothing but sponge baths since I woke up—and probably for a long time before that—a shower sounds like a small slice of heaven.

"I'll be right here," the Master says, releasing me with a small smile.

It feels like a benediction.

Lucía hustles me to the bathroom with that gentle-yet-firm way the nurses have. I try to cooperate, and my unsteady legs are waking up, so we make it inside, and she closes the door.

"Arms up!" she says, showing me by example like maybe I've forgotten how.

"I can get it off." But when I try, she has to help me anyway. My limbs all have a certain awkwardness to them like they've forgotten how to bend or fold or do the hundred motions one does without thinking but which apparently atrophy away when you lie in bed for weeks on end.

Lucía starts the shower and steam fills the room. I work off my panties, which fall to the floor, and I let her get them only because I'm not sure what to do. Or whether my balance is any good.

"Okay, dear." Her hand is in the spray, testing it for me. "You can do this. But you need to use the handholds. Don't make Lucía come in after you and mess up my pretty hair." She jauntily pats her utilitarian updo, long deep-brown hair pragmatically tied up in a bun.

"You're very nice to me, Lucía." I grab the handhold outside the shower and step inside while she holds back the curtain. The warm spray prickles my skin as I ease into it.

"Now, just take a seat," she instructs then waits until I settle on the smooth plastic protruding from the wall. It's chilly on my bare bottom but heating quickly. "Everything you need is on the shelf, okay?

Shampoo. Soap. I will be right back. No acrobatics, *sí?*"

"No acrobatics," I promise.

"That's my girl."

Before she can draw the curtain to give me privacy, I ask, "How long have you been taking care of me, Lucía?"

She stops and gives me a kind look. "How long have you been asleep, *tía*, or how long have you been awake?"

"Yes." I let my eyes plead with her.

"Two days since you woke up," she says, more serious now. "Three weeks before that."

I nod.

She smiles and draws the curtain.

I carefully soap up my whole body. I'm usually on the lean side, but my arms and legs are painfully thin. Part of that's the starvation while being tortured by the elves. Part is sitting in that bed in an apparent coma. *Three weeks.* Thank the Universe I had some muscle-tone before all this, due to my handy work. Running up and down ladders, hauling around my toolbelt, hanging curtains and painting doors... all of it built up strength that feels like a memory now. I take a deep breath and hold onto the shower's handrail to haul myself up from the seat. Standing full in the spray now, I let it cascade over me, rinsing away the soap and drenching my hair. I give it a good washing, but that takes all the energy I have left. I sit back down before I earn Lucía's ire. She returns with a towel and helps me dry off. She's brought new clothes too, but they're folded and wrapped in a ribbon, which seems strange.

Lucía notices my stare as she helps me with my panties. "Those are from your boyfriend."

I whip a look to her.

She shrugs as she tugs my panties up into place. "Or whoever *Señor* Hottie is."

I laugh a little. The Master is undeniably beautiful. I realize how ridiculous it is that I don't know his name. "He's just watching out for me."

She stands and picks up the wrapped clothes, cocking a skeptical eyebrow. As she unwraps the ribbon, I see it's a dress similar but not identical to the one I was wearing while captured—a simple, spaghetti-strap white-linen thing that's probably less substantial than the nightgowns I've been cycling through. It occurs to me those weren't the kind any hospital carries as stock-issue. He's been providing me clothes all long.

"I could be wrong," Lucía says as she bunches

up the dress to slip over my head. "But this is not the present of a man who wishes only to be friends."

I see what she means as it slides into place. It's really two layers—a solid sheath underneath and a more diaphanous layer that floats on top. The top dips down enough to be slightly sexy in an innocent way while the skirt is short enough to expose a whole lot of leg above the knee. The sundress I wore while captive was simple and utilitarian. Plain cotton and simple construction. The best part of it was the flowing skirt, which felt freeing after wearing my normal, heavier work pants and shirts all week long. But it wasn't *feminine* the way this one is.

Lucía towels my hair as I peer down at the dress. "Your brush is by your bed," she says. "Let's go get you settled."

"I'd like to stay awake for a while." I'm *exhausted,* but I don't want to fall back asleep right away. I have questions. And not for Lucía.

"Sure, *tía.*" She swings open the bathroom door, and I emerge with bare feet, towel-dried hair, and this dress that moves when I walk, creating a rippling flow around my legs. I actually like it, a lot. But it's so pretty and delicate—unusual for me.

The Master scrambles to his feet, his eyes drinking me in.

That flush covers my entire body.

"I will check back on you later, *tía!*" Lucía sings on her way out the door.

It closes behind her.

The Master is hurrying over to offer his arm, but I hold up a hand to stop him. "I just want to sit for a while."

He hesitates then goes back for the plastic chair he was sitting in. I take a seat facing the bed. I expect him to stand or find a seat on the bed opposite me, but instead, he goes to the dresser and rummages in the top drawer. I close my eyes and rest for a moment, just breathing and sitting upright without support. A simple shower was exhausting. How long will it take me to recover from this? The nurses have said I'm a miracle case—they don't know why I was in a coma, and they don't know why I'm not in one now. They're not treating me for anything but exhaustion. At some point, I should be able to leave. It's hard to think that far ahead.

Suddenly, a hand is on my shoulder.

My eyes fly open.

The Master is behind me. His hand slips into my hair, and something tugs on it—gently. It takes me a moment to realize: *he's brushing my hair.* His hands are strong but infinitely careful. He's running his fingers through the long strands, finger-combing them, then following with a bristled brush I glimpse out the corner of my eye. His strokes are slow and luxurious, and he cradles my head to counter the motion. It's like a scalp massage and hair brushing all in one. I close my eyes, letting him move me as he wishes. Then just as suddenly, his hands slip away.

I open my eyes again, but before I can turn to look, a rumbling sound starts up behind me. *A hairdryer.* His hands are back in my hair again, lifting the still-wet locks away and blowing the hot air across them. I close my eyes again, just enjoying the touch and heat. Every inch of my skin is goose-bumped from the contrast of the hot air and cold traces of wet hair across my back.

What is happening here? Am I being the Fool once again, letting the cards lead me into trusting a man I don't even know? There's a sexual promise in this slow, careful tending. In the loose yet suggestive dress. I've had lovers before, on occasion, and I'm not oblivious to the warmup signals and sexual tension that seem to spring from nowhere between people. The Lovers card speaks to the essential duality of love—between the *Lover* and the *Beloved.* I thought the Emperor card was beckoning me to follow, to finally meet that purpose the Universe had yet in store for me.

Maybe it was just what my mind needed to conjure at that moment. To wake up.

The hairdryer cuts off. My hair is weightless now, soft and gently floating about my shoulders. The Master gives it several more strokes with the brush, and then he comes around and kneels in front of me and the chair, bristle brush still in hand, his eyes glowing and earnest as he peers up at me.

"Thank you," he breathes. A small smile sneaks out. "For allowing that."

"Who *are* you?" A question I should have asked long ago.

Again, torment fills his face that I don't understand. "I want to tell you," he says, "but I don't think you'll believe me."

My hands are gripping my knees, just below the hem of this short skirt. Now that I'm sitting, I realize how revealing it is. My arms are locked, a defensive shield of sorts, against the powerful card he is. "Because you're made of magic."

The shock opens his expression, but he quickly recovers. "You remember."

"Of course, I remember." Am I not supposed to remember the torture I endured at the hands of magical creatures? Or the endless waiting, hovering between the realms? I remember my *past* lives— recalling what's just happened in this one is not a stretch. My agitation is making my arms shake. I grip my knees harder. "Tell me who you are," I demand, more harshly this time, because my greatest fear at this point is that I haven't broken free of being the Fool. That my urge to regain my child-like innocence, before I knew of evil magic in the world, has led me to put trust in yet another dangerous man. He's refusing to answer, so I put it more plainly. "Are you in league with them? The ones who tortured me?"

"*No!*" It's so forceful and sudden, breaking through whatever torment he has, that I'm compelled to believe him.

"Then what?" I press. "Because those beings were made of magic, and you haven't denied that you are as well." *And I've seen you.* I might mistake a card's meaning, but I can't conjure a being out of nothingness. I'd never seen this man before he appeared in the card above the lake. *That means something.* It has to.

"All right." He stands up from where he was

kneeling in front of me and takes a seat on the bed, a little further away. I narrow my eyes. He suddenly needs distance for this? Why? "My people are dragons. We can take human form, but we are not human. We were nearly wiped out two hundred years ago by the dark elves—the Vardigah—who tortured you. They hunt us still."

I nod because this makes perfect sense. "Why do they hate you?"

He gives an elaborate, open-palmed shrug. "We're ancient enemies, the source of the conflict lost to time. For thousands of years, before even our recorded history, there was a separate race of elves —the light elves—who kept the Vardigah contained. Or at least kept them from attacking us. Then one day, they nearly wiped us from the face of the earth."

"Two hundred years ago." A long-standing war. He's the Emperor, after all. Sometimes, the cards are literal. That can be the most surprising turn of all.

"You're taking this extraordinarily well." The look on his face is almost comical.

I scowl at him. "I was psychically tortured by dark elves." I mentally high-five myself for guessing what they were correctly. "Vicious magical creatures attempted to break my soul. The fact that you're a dragon is not exactly *strange* by comparison."

He nods, but it's tentative, and his expression is still bound up in surprise.

Trickles of fear are working through my body, pooling at the bottom of my stomach. "Why me?" I whisper. "I'm not one of you. How did I get caught up in your war?" *And why are you here?* I also want to ask. But I'm not sure if he'll tell me the truth now. And I'm feeling the Fool even more for trusting him at all.

He leans forward, giving me a soft look. "They tried, and nearly succeeded, to find every human woman who was destined to be our mates. They wanted to break you in order to destroy us."

I lean back. *Mates?* "I don't understand."

His shoulders drop. There's a certain terror in his eyes that makes me reflexively fold my arms in front of me and draw my knees closer on the chair. "You're my soul mate," he says. "Your soul and mine are two halves of a single soul. If they could destroy yours, I would perish as well. And that is the Vardigah's goal. To wipe us from the planet."

I blink. My mouth slowly falls open. The shock feels like I'm made of glass that's suddenly shattered and avalanched down into a pile at my feet. *It's truth.* I can feel it. But I can't even begin to wrap my mind about what that *means.*

My head is shaking *no* before I can even form words.

"Daisy, I—" But he stops at the horror on my face.

My hands itch for my cards. If I could do a clean draw—an honest draw, not one depending on my untrustworthy imagination, my Fool-ish nature —maybe I could understand the meaning of this. See a path through all of it. But right now, it's too much.

My body unfolds from the chair. I move past him to climb onto my bed. The blanket is thin, and the sheet is too, barely any warmth in this suddenly cold room.

I burrow under them anyway, drawing them up to my chin. My back is turned to him. He's risen from the bed, and I hear the sigh, even though he tries to keep it quiet. I don't hear his footfalls, but I sense him moving away like there's some tether between us that's being stretched.

The sound of the door opening jolts me. I turn under the covers and fling out my hand. "Wait!"

He pauses at the door, his face stricken.

"Don't leave," I mumble. My hand's trembling,

so I draw it back under the covers. Then I turn away again because I can't explain it. I don't know why I would try to make him stay.

The door closes again, but I know he's on this side of it. I hear the chair scrape as he takes a seat.

I close my eyes and let myself escape into the darkness of sleep.

FOUR

Akkan

I'VE SPENT A LIFETIME DREAMING OF THIS.

Meeting my soul mate. Making it sweet. Earning her love. I've spent the last few weeks half in despair that she'd never awaken, half in terror she would—and I'd blow the entire thing.

That second half knew me better.

Somehow, I'm completely fouling all of it. Yet… she told me not to leave. A tiny flame of hope still sputters in my soul. Maybe it's not too late to fix this. Daisy's sleeping hard, going on twenty hours now. Meals have come and gone. I tried dozing in the chair but discovered long ago that was impossible. I left for a short while to try sleeping in the visitor's lounge, but it was nothing but fitful nightmares of her hand slipping from mine as she fell off a cliff.

It's morning again, back in the room. She's still curled up in the dress I brought, huddled under the blankets like they might shield her from reality.

A reality I dumped on her like a metric ton of wet cement.

I should have waited. That she believed every word caught me off guard. That she so thoroughly accepted the unimaginable lured me into thinking that maybe my luck had finally turned. That all this waiting would finally pay off, and *something* would go right in this arena of my life. I've loved other women—I know relationships are never easy, that you have to work at them—but having my literal other half before me raises the stakes... and the promise. It has me off-balance, terrified of the return of that pain, the one that's shadowed me all my life. *Devastating Loss*. Losing Daisy, or simply having her turn me away, will hurt like nothing else has. And I already *know* what it's like to lose everything and everyone.

I'm gazing out the window at the threatening early-morning rain when I hear her move.

She stretches, her bare toes slipping out of the covers as she elongates her body, eyes still closed. She's a beautiful woman—that goes without saying —but she's still so thin. Maybe this is her normal shape, but I fear the ravages of the Vardigah have marked her. I've felt the weakness in her arms the few times she's let me help. But when she opens her eyes, they're clear. Her face has more color in it every day. *Patience, Akkan.* The poor woman is still recovering bodily from a terrible trauma.

I smile when she sees me. "Still here," I say, opening the possibility that I'll leave if she wants. It would kill me, but I'd do it—if only so she knows I'll respect whatever she decides. I'm not a *curse* upon her. At least, I don't want to be.

She nods, sits up, and rubs her eyes. The last meal is still here—she scoots to the edge of the bed, her back to me, and lifts the cover to check it out.

"I can order you something fresh." I tentatively move closer. I have no idea what our status is.

She unwraps the plastic-covered fork and pokes at the cold eggs. "What's your name?" She asks it without turning, without looking at me.

But I take it as an invitation, quickly stepping around the bed so I can face her. "Akkan."

"Is that a dragon name?" She flicks a look at me, then forks up some eggs and puts them in her mouth.

"Akkan is not that unusual for a dragon of my time. I'm from Greece, but the name itself has some

Turkish roots. My full name is Akkan Nikanor Azarchehr."

She raises her eyebrows, still chewing.

"It's a mouthful," I say with a smirk. My heart is thudding, but she's not throwing me out. Yet.

"Akkan." She says my name like she's trying it on for size. I can't tell if it pleases her or not. She spears more eggs. "So, the other half of my soul is a dragon from Greece." She flicks a look at me but then keeps her gaze trained on her food. "How does that work, exactly? And what do you mean, *'a dragon of my time'?"*

I take it as a further invitation and snag the plastic chair, turning it backward to sit facing her across the tray. She's up higher than I am, perched on her hospital bed, but I'm taller, so we're about level. "I was born in 1795."

Her fork freezes momentarily on the way to her mouth. She looks to see if I'm serious, which I am, so she continues eating. She waits for me to explain, so I do.

"Dragons live a long time, but I'm near the end of mine."

That grabs her attention. She looks me over, studying me. "You look about my age. Forty. Maybe a little older."

"As I will until I start the Withering." I grimace. How to explain this without driving her away with talk of mating? "It's what happens at the end of our lives. The magic finally fails, and death comes swiftly. It's a mercy that way, I suppose."

She nods and returns to her food, picking up some toast and taking a big bite. I'm actually pleased to see her appetite returning—it's been so weakened, like the rest of her. But when she finishes that bite, she sets it down and shoves away the whole thing. Her hair is wonderfully mussed, and her dress is hiked up nearly to her panties. She doesn't fix any of it, just holds me with a serious stare that captivates me.

"What does this mean, being soul mates?" she asks. "You said we're connected in some way. That the Vardigah could get to you through me."

I swallow. I guess there's no way around it. "When I was born, my dragon soul was broken and half fused with your human soul. We call you *dragon spirited*. If the Vardigah had succeeded in destroying your dragon soul, I would have simply died. But you would have lived on."

"So that's why you're here." She's studying me again. "To make sure the half I'm carrying doesn't get destroyed."

"No." I cringe again, but I feel the need to be honest with her. "I'm here because our souls are meant to be together."

She scowls. "Soul mates."

"Yes." I bite my lip, waiting for the backlash.

"I don't understand." She shakes her head then looks down at her mostly bare legs. She purses her lips, eases down from the bed, then straightens the skirt, so it falls farther. What was I thinking, getting her something so obviously sensual? It's making her uncomfortable. "So, what?" She props her hands on her hips and stares at me, defiant. "We're supposed to be lovers? Is that it?"

Obviously not happening any time this century. I hold out my hands, palm up. "I only wanted to make sure you were okay, Daisy. I don't expect…" I lean back and run both hands through my hair. "I'm sorry." I stand up from the chair, and it skids forward a little. "Of course, not," I finally answer her question. "You don't know me. You've been kidnapped and tortured *because* of me. Why would you ever be interested in…" My distress is leaking into my voice, and I don't want that either. I press my hands together and hold them in front of my face, closing my eyes and breathing in some reservoir of calm. It takes a moment, but decades of training come through. When I open my eyes again, she's staring at me with a newly open expression. "You're the other half of my soul, Daisy. I couldn't *not* make sure you were okay. I couldn't *not* care that you were safe and recovering from the things you suffered, things for which I'm responsible even though I couldn't stop it. I didn't even know—" Again, the stab of ancient pain. I breathe through that as well. "I'm here to make sure you're okay."

Her chin lifts, studying me anew. I'm discovering she has a piercing gaze when she wishes, and I'm right now in that blazing light.

At that moment, the door swings open, and the nurse bustles in. There are so many different ones, but this is the one who I entrusted to give Daisy the dress she's wearing now.

"Miss Daisy!" Lucía proclaims. "Good—you're awake!" She brushes past me and wheels over the small stand with the blood pressure cuff. "Just need to take your vitals, but this is your lucky day, *tía!*"

"How's that?" But Daisy complies, taking a seat while Lucía wraps the cuff around her thin arm.

"Today, you're gonna get to go home!" The nurse gives me a small smile like I'm in on some joke, but I'm absolutely not.

I look to Daisy.

"Oh," she says, but her cheeks have gone more pale than normal.

"That is okay, right?" Lucía asks. "That is what you want?" Again, she peeks at me, but this time her expression is more uncertain.

"Sure," Daisy says, but it doesn't sound like the truth. "Akkan, can you do something for me?"

"Of course." My mind is reeling. I hadn't thought this far ahead, but I'm completely unwilling to let her go. At the same time, I realize that's not up to me. My heart lurches into panic.

"I want to talk to my friends." Daisy's watching Lucía listen to her heart. "Grace and Jayda." She looks to me. "Can you tell them? I don't have a phone." Lucía presses a thermometer to her forehead.

I nod and pull out my phone, texting them quickly. It's morning here in New York. Grace is still in the Greek Isles with Theo, and Jayda should be in the south of France with her mate, Ree, but it shouldn't be too late for them to stop by. There are many advantages to being a mated dragon, but tele-portation has to be one of the most extraordinary. I've never understood why that was part of the package. Enhanced dragon powers like venom and strength, I can understand—that's just more of what every dragon is born with. But teleportation? It's always struck me as odd. More so now, in the modern age. Back when I was a young dragon, naïve to the ways of the world, it was just another magic that belonged to the mated ones.

When I look up from my phone, Lucía's finished with her vitals check.

"All right, Miss Daisy," she says, cheerily, "you're doing great. The doctor just has to sign off on the discharge order. I know you're a strong one, honey, but you should have someone at home to watch over you for a while, okay?" She gives me a meaningful look, but then turns and bustles out of the room, off to her next patient.

Daisy is frowning at her hands, which are back to gripping her knees as she sits on the edge of the bed.

"Do you…" I stall out. It's never occurred to me before. I've been so wrapped up in caring for her… but she could have a boyfriend. A husband? Surely, she would have mentioned it. Right? "I don't know where you live, Daisy." I just leave it at that.

She narrows her eyes. "I was staying with a friend." Then she's up out of bed and searching the room, checking out the dresser.

My heart is sinking. What friend? It's probably

already hopeless with her, but if she's involved with someone—

"Where's my stuff?" she demands as she cycles through the dresser a second time.

"We had to get rid of everything."

She whips her head to me. "What?"

I look to the door, but Lucía has closed it behind her. Still, I lower my voice. "The Vardigah track by *things.* Anything you were wearing while you were captured, they'd be able to find you again using that. So, I destroyed all of it. I'm sorry."

She just blinks, and her face loses its color.

"You're safe now, I promise." I want to reassure her with my touch, but it's not really welcome. I gesture to her white, filmy dress. "I tried to find something that would be similar. I'm sorry if it wasn't the right thing."

She frowns down at the dress and smooths it across her belly. She's still so thin from the starvation and the coma, it hangs on her. "It's fine." It almost sounds like she means it.

The door swings open suddenly—Jayda and Grace stride in.

"Holy shit, you're up!" Grace gushes. She hurries across the room. I step out of the way just as she grabs Daisy into a hug.

Shock lights up Daisy's face as she hugs Grace back. "How did you get here so fast?"

Grace ignores that as Jayda tugs her aside. "Don't hog the girl, Grace." Then Jayda wraps her arms around Daisy and hugs her as well. "Oh, *Lord*, it's good to see you upright."

A smile is finally showing up on Daisy's face. She pulls back and looks between the two of them. "Don't tell me you've been camping outside my door all this time!"

"Um." Jayda pulls back and exchanges a look with Grace. "We were nearby."

I step over to the door and close it. "She knows," I tell them.

"All of it?" Grace asks, eyes wide.

"What do I know?" Daisy asks, clearly not happy.

I join the three of them in the center of the room. "That dragons exist. That we mate with our soul mates. And that the Vardigah track you through your things. The teleportation is new to her." I nod to Jayda and Grace. "As is your status."

"Teleportation?" Daisy asks them, incredulous. "Is he serious?"

"Well, only if you're *mated,*" Grace says with a smirk.

Jayda glares at her.

Grace's eyes go wide. "Oops."

Jayda sighs.

Daisy's nodding like teleportation is, of course, the natural thing that comes along with a magic world of dragons and elves. And she's already on to the next thing. "You two are soul mates. Like me. And you've…" She flicks a very concerned look at me then at her friends. "You're *mated*? Already? What does that even mean? And when did this happen?"

"You were sleeping, honey." Jayda gives a small shrug. "Although, to be fair, it all happened pretty fast."

Grace is biting her lip, keeping quiet now that she's spilled everything. I'm not sure that it matters. Daisy's earlier easy acceptance of all things magical *obviously* doesn't extend to embracing that I'm her soul mate. My heart is still doing battle with what that means, but I need to keep my focus on making sure she's cared for. If she'll allow it. The rest matters little anyway.

Daisy's gaze is flitting between the three of us. "You knew. You all knew all along about all of this." Then her gaze becomes untethered from us and wanders around the room.

"You were only just recovering," I try. "No one wanted to rush you."

Jayda angles to get her attention again. "Daisy, honey, it's a lot. We weren't hiding it from you. We just knew that…" She glances at me, which makes me cringe. "Well, that you were in good hands."

Daisy's gaze sharpens with that. "Because Akkan's my soul mate."

"Well… yes." Jayda seems to realize there's a problem. Too late.

Daisy edges past all of us to return to the bed and the tray with her half-eaten food. She looks down at her dress again and her bare feet. The vulnerability of it has me cursing myself and wishing I'd just kept with the plain pajamas I'd been supplying. This dress is my fantasy running ahead of me.

Suddenly, the door opens, and Lucía pops her head in. "Miss Daisy! The doctor will be here with the discharge papers in a moment, okay? Just wanted to let you know." She sweeps a look over all of us but then retreats.

Daisy turns back to us. "You can go," she says to all three of us. "I can take care of myself."

"*What?*" Grace gasps.

"Oh, hell no." Jayda steps forward. I've only just

met the woman recently, but I can tell she's a *tour de force*. "You can come back home with me. You need someone to watch over you until you're feeling better." Jayda throws a quick pointed look at me, but I'm not going to interfere.

"Or you can stay with Theo and me," Grace adds, sliding between Jayda and the tray of food. "We're honeymooning on the Greek Isles, and you wouldn't believe it—" She cuts off at Jayda's scowl. "What?"

Daisy eases onto the bed and looks defeated. But when she looks up at her friends, her voice is nothing but kindness. "You two…" She shakes her head. "I knew the Universe had plans for you. I didn't know *specifically* it was mating with dragons, but the Universe is tricky that way. But I'm not going to move in on your honeymoons."

"It's not like that…" Grace starts then bites her lip.

Jayda leans into Daisy and says in a mock whisper, "It's *totally* like that."

Daisy smiles. And for that alone, I'm grateful her friends are here.

Jayda puts on a serious face. "Look, we can get someone to stay with you at your apartment—a nurse, or something." She flicks a look at me like she expects me to lean into this. But I've already screwed things up.

Daisy sighs. "I don't, technically, have an apartment."

Grace frowns. "Where were you staying before? You never did tell us."

Daisy shrugs one shoulder while staring at her bare feet. "I stay with friends. Move around. You know, whoever will let me use their couch for a while." She pulls in a breath and looks up. "I'm handy. *Task Rabbit* brings in enough for food and basics. Just not enough for rent in the city, you know?"

Jayda's face is drawing down with concern, but relief is filling me—the *friend* is simply a friend. Maybe even less.

Grace looks confused. "What's Task Rabbit?"

"It's a gig economy thing, Rich Girl," Jayda chastises her lightly. To Daisy, she says, "You can stay at my apartment in the city. I never use it anymore. Well, almost never."

"I don't want to put you out—"

"You should stay with me." I say it with the assurance that I'm finally feeling. I haven't even figured out *where* yet, but the *with me* part is necessary, now that I know there's no one else who's staked a claim to her heart.

Grace and Jayda hold their breath and look to Daisy to see her response. Her eyes are fixed on me, that scrutinizing stare again. So, I make my pitch. "I'm your soul mate. You need someone to watch over you until you're recovered. I'm going to be doing it anyway, Daisy." I gesture to the chair I've been occupying. "I've been doing it for weeks. It's just a matter of whether you'll let me help you or whether I'll be camped out across the street, texting you relentlessly to make sure you're okay."

A flicker of a smile crosses her face. "I don't have a phone."

"We can fix that." I hold that brown-eyed stare of hers.

Uncertainty clouds her expression, and she drops her gaze. "I need my things. My Tarot deck. My tools." Then fatigue seems to take over, drawing down her shoulders.

I edge forward, Jayda and Grace backing up to give me room, and I kneel on one knee next to the bed. "They took you because of me. I'm not going to rest until your life is put back together, Daisy. Whatever that takes."

Her expression opens. "The Emperor builds a better world."

I frown and glance at Jayda and Grace. They seem baffled as well.

I turn back to Daisy. "I'll build a better world for you, I promise."

She nods, and it's an acceptance that floods my heart and lifts me up. Just as I rise, there's a knock at the door, and the doctor enters. I step back to let him check her and clear her for discharge, but my mind is whirling ahead.

I need a home for my mate.

FIVE

Daisy

THE *MAGIC* OF ALL THIS IS SINKING IN.

First, the teleportation. Grace is *mated*—whatever that truly means—so she was able to teleport Akkan and me from the stairwell of the hospital to this inexpressibly beautiful seaside cottage on an island called Hydra, which is near Athens. *Greece.* Grace brought us halfway around the world in a blink. Which is good because I was exhausted just making it to the stairwell. Once we arrived, Akkan parked me in an oversized wicker chair with a nest of cushions and blankets and a beautiful view of a quiet port and the sparkling blue sea. Grace assured me, with a wink, this wasn't *her* honeymoon cottage, then she whisked Akkan back to the city to gather my things.

That's the second part of the magic. *Akkan.* He's truly the Emperor card come to life, but not in the way I thought. He's kind and caring with a depth of soul I can see in his eyes. The worst part of the Vardigah was discovering the world of magic was evil. But Akkan is the *good* kind of magic—the kind I've always thought was the natural way of the Universe.

But this business about being soul mates?

I can accept that I'm holding onto half of his dragon soul—my lives have always been complicated, not quite of this world. And there's a connection between us, if only the intense way he looks at me with those pretty slate-blue eyes. There's plenty to like about the man. He's as beautiful as the quaint Greek village that is my view. It's almost evening here, and the sun is lowering in the sky, turning it a dragon-fire orange. I can accept that Akkan feels some obligation to care for me, and this is his way of doing that. But this business of *mating?* He didn't seem to take any slight when I wanted to change back into the soft cotton pajamas. It's clear I'm in no shape for sexual adventures. Men are something I indulge in on occasion when the itch strikes. Or there's particular chemistry. We enjoy each other for a time, and then I set them free. The

Lovers card was never one I drew for any length of time.

I'm not here for a honeymoon.

And yet... is this the destiny the Universe has been holding out for me? To be a dragon's mate? It feels otherworldly and strange—*magical*—but what does it even mean?

I need my deck. The real one I've been itching for all this time. The cards will show me the way. They're the one constant, the one thing I trust. People have never been steady enough or reliable enough, but the cards have never steered me wrong. I settle back in my chair and wait. Just as I'm drifting off, Akkan returns, laden with several bags of stuff, Grace's hand on his shoulder. She lets go of him and then disappears.

I frown—I didn't get a chance to say goodbye. "Did she leave for good?"

"Just going for food." Akkan brushes me with a look that feels a little too intimate, but I can't decide if that's my imagination. "Are you all right?" He's still carrying the stuff.

"I'm fine." I perk up a little. "Did you find my cards?"

He smiles and hurries to set down the things— they look mostly like clothes, my tool bag, and a few toiletries; I travel light—then pulls my deck from one bag. When he hands it over, I just cradle it in my hands a moment. The High Priestess graces the box, which is worn at the corners, but her cascading red hair and eyelids painted as faux all-seeing eyes are still vibrant.

"Thank you," I say and mean it. Just holding them gives me a sense of center I haven't had since I was taken. A light shudder runs through me with that thought.

"Are you cold?" he asks, concern furrowing his brow.

That he noticed feels both too personal and strangely reassuring. I peer up at him. "Just kind of… overwhelmed? And I'm afraid I may disappoint you as a soul mate, Akkan. I'm not very up for romance at the moment."

His concern melts away, and he kneels in front of my chair. He keeps doing that, and I find it oddly touching. He's an Emperor, at least in some sense— a leader in his world, I imagine. Yet he's at pains to lower himself down to my level, whatever that might be.

He lifts a blanket hanging over the side of the chair and gently lays it across my curled-up legs. He tucks it in by my feet, then lifts his gaze. "You have no idea how long I've waited just to be able to look into your eyes."

I smile. "Three weeks? Lucía said I was out that long."

"So much longer than that."

My smile fades. "I don't know about this—"

"Don't." He lays his hand on my two, still clutching my cards. "Just let me care for you, okay? That's the only arrangement we have here. I get to make sure you're safe and have whatever you need. You heal from the trauma of all this. That's all I need." He seems to genuinely mean it.

I settle a little more into the chair. "I can do that."

Akkan scurries off with my things to another room. The cottage itself is beautiful in its simplicity. White plaster walls with blue painted-wood-trimmed windows overlooking the water. The ceiling is rough-hewn wooden beams, and the floor is white-washed wood of the same kind. A rattan couch sits opposite my chair, and there's a small coffee table between, but the rest of the cozy room is just a tiny table with an empty vase and stylish lamp. Around the corner, I can glimpse marble counters and hanging herbs and pots—looks like a gourmet kitchen. Akkan went down the other hallway to what probably is bedrooms. Or perhaps a single one. Despite his assurances, that still concerns me.

Just as he returns, empty-handed, Grace arrives carrying two large bags. "I have food!" she proclaims, handing them over to Akkan. "Stuffed tomatoes and peppers, souvlaki, fried zucchini balls, Greek salad… you two have a feast!"

"Thank you, Grace," he says.

"You just take care of my girl, all right?" She scowls at him, but it's playful. Then she comes over and gives me a hug. "If you need anything— anything at all—I want you to promise you'll have Akkan text me, okay?"

"Promise."

She gives me one more hug, then waves and disappears.

Teleportation. I'm still getting used to that magic.

Akkan lifts the food bags. The mixed aromas are already filling the room. "Hungry?"

"Not just yet," I say. "Maybe later?"

He nods and whisks those away, heading to the kitchen.

I bask in the quiet warmth of the cottage. The sky is turning redder as the sun sinks. The distant sound of seagulls searching for their dinner floats through the open window along with the port's salty air. My box of Tarot cards still sits cradled in my hands. I open it and pull out the deck. Normally, I'd use the full set—both major and minor arcana—but I'm in need of powerful guidance, and my mind is tired, so I sort out the major arcana and stow the rest. As I shuffle, just a simple overhand mixing of the cards, Akkan returns with two steaming mugs. He sets them on the coffee table and takes a seat on the sofa opposite me.

"I took the liberty of making some *tsai*—Greek tea." He has a small smile as he cradles his earthen mug in his hands and blows to cool it. "It's just chamomile, but it's considered a cure-all for anything that ails you."

I can't help but be charmed. "I'll take any curing you've got." My face runs a little hot when I realize how open-ended that sounds. "Especially tea," I add, unfolding my legs and leaning forward to pick up the mug. It's warm, but not too hot—I take a few sips, and it seems like there must be magic in it already because everything in me loosens a little and relaxes.

Akkan's watching me intensely, but not so it makes me uncomfortable. He lifts his chin to the cards still in my hand. "Are you going to do a reading for me?"

"I usually read for myself." I set the mug back on the table.

He seems intrigued. "Can I watch? Or will that ruin it?"

I smile. "It is a little personal. But I don't mind." Maybe a good reading will help settle this arrangement we have and where it's going… and where it is *not*. That's the question I want to pose to the cards anyway. I shuffle them a few more times, then draw three, placing them face down on the table.

"Past, present, future," I say, tapping the center of each card and setting the rest of the deck aside. "Or, if I'm doing a more centering draw, I would say *Release, Begin, Sustain. Release* will tell me something I need to leave behind. *Begin* tells of something I need to start. And *Sustain* shows something good that I need to get back to my sustaining center."

He's very interested. "I thought the cards told the future."

"Tarot helps you tap into your subconscious, drawing out your higher being and connecting you with the Universe. If you're centered and understand your purpose, the future will unfold as it should." I don't mention I've been searching for my purpose my entire life… or that I wonder if being a dragon's mate is it. I pull my legs back up into the rattan chair and rest my hands on my folded knees. I focus on the three cards spread on the table then close my eyes. I breathe in and silently meditate on the question I've posed to the cards ever since I started readings. *What's my purpose?* Usually, I mean it in a more specific sense—what's my next step here, right now, to lead me to the higher purpose the Universe has for me? Today, the question is framed around this idea of being a dragon's mate. Specifically, *this* dragon's mate. Am I supposed to allow this handsome man into my life, or is Akkan simply a bridge to somewhere else I'm supposed to go? I don't trust easily—doubly so for men—so I'm looking for a serious sign from the cards.

When I open my eyes, Akkan has a faint smile on his face. "You meditate."

"I'm focusing my intention so I can connect with the cards."

He gestures for me to proceed, but his eyes are bright with curiosity.

It is strange to do a reading as a performance like this. I've done it before with friends, or even acquaintances looking for guidance on how it works, but not usually with a complete stranger. Although Akkan's been at my bedside for three days since I've woken up and three weeks while I was out —he's really not a stranger. I push that awkwardness aside and focus my intent.

Is my purpose to be a dragon's mate?

I turn over the first card. *The Hermit.* A woman seated but floating in the air on a burst of magic and stardust. She looks out over the ocean, white rocky cliffs and a staircase cut in stone below her. My gaze is drawn to the real-life window of this cottage in the Greek Isles and the white craggy stone cliffs all around the port. Akkan looks between the card and the window as well.

"Are you the hermit?" he asks.

"The Hermit is the past." I'm more than a bit unnerved by the similarity between the card and myself, even down to how far I am above the water, the fact that I'm facing it, and even my pose in the chair. All right, cards, I get it. *This cottage is the hermitage.* My time here is limited. "The Hermit spends time alone in contemplation. She's withdrawn from the world, seeking inner wisdom. This is my past. This is what I must release. I have to return to the world."

"You've already taken great strides in that." He

means to encourage, but he's breaking my flow. "You emerged from a three-week coma. Might take some time to fully recover from that."

I narrow my eyes. "Are you doing this reading, or am I?"

He laughs lightly then cocks his head, grinning. "My apologies. Please continue."

I wonder if his sexy smile lets him get away with everything. I think perhaps the answer is yes.

I return to the card, tapping it once. "The Hermit can be physical, mental, or spiritual. Maybe it's the coma I've already left behind. Maybe it's this cottage that I should leave." I flick a look at him, a bit of a challenge, and watch the smirk fade from his face. "Or maybe it's an emotional apartness that I should release, emerging from isolation to rejoin the world of other people." I'm thinking of my friends and clients back in the city. No one close, although a couple probably wonder where I disappeared to. Not enough to report me missing or anything. Jayda and Grace are probably the closest friends I've ever had. Which could be a sad commentary on my life, but attachments aren't something I've fostered in this lifetime. Not since I was on my own.

Just one more reason to be skeptical that the Universe wants me to be anyone's "mate."

"The second card," I say, tapping it before I turn, "is the present. If the past is what I should *Release*, this is something I should *Begin*. It's the path to wellbeing in the present moment." I turn the card.

The Lovers.

Everything in me stills.

The card is richly sensuous. A couple embracing, naked and nearly kissing. Their eyes are closed, her hair whipping around in the storm of their intimacy. His hair is bundled in dreadlocks behind him, but she's grabbed hold of some, pulling him into the embrace. Passionate red and swirls of magic surround them.

"The Lovers are…" I stall out and slowly drag my gaze up to meet Akkan's.

His eyes are blazing.

"It's… a duality," I mumble then drop my gaze to the card again. "Two halves of a whole. Soul mates." My throat is running dry. "A great amount of trust is required for a lasting bond. Vulnerability, honesty…" I stop. It's shaking me to the core. My resistance to this card is *fierce*, but the Universe is pulling no punches with me today.

"You *are* my soul mate, Daisy," he says softly. "The cards are correct about that. But that doesn't mean you're bound to anything. You get to choose."

My gaze snaps up. "Do I?" I've never felt like I was the captain of my own fate. The tempest of the Universe tossed me where it wanted me to go, and I did my best to ride the waves without breaking.

"Yes, you do." He's certain of this. "With me, in any case."

And I believe him. At least, I believe he means it.

I blink and stare down at the third card. "The *Future.* This is the possibility before me. The thing I need to *Sustain* my forward movement." Toward my purpose. In a way, I'm glad I drew the Lovers first. Maybe that's something for right now, but I'm moving through this present moment into a Future that's something other than being Akkan's lover. I turn the card.

Death.

My throat closes up.

To be precise, *Death and Rebirth.* The duality of this card is shown in the darkened red hood, so much like the Reaper, but instead of a face, there's a shining star within. To make it more complex, the card is in reversal—upside down. I rarely read reversals, especially for major arcana. The cards are powerful in their own right, holding all the meanings simultaneously, but this time… it feels like the Universe is telling me something more.

"Daisy?" Akkan's voice is even softer.

I clear my throat. "Death and Rebirth. The reversal means the card is blocked. Or Rebirth is dominant. But some transformation or symbolic death is coming. It's a metamorphosis. An expansion that moves you closer to your most divine essence." I've never read the Death card literally, but having just spent weeks in torture and then the eternal lake, floating and hovering between the real world and the magical one… the Grim Reaper's breath feels too close to the back of my neck. I shiver and gather the blankets Akkan has heaped around me. He's up from the couch and once again kneeling before me.

"You're not going to die," he says. "I'll make sure of that."

I give a small, mirthless laugh. "I've already survived the worst the Vardigah could throw at me."

"Exactly right." His eyes are bright. And kind. "You're strong. You've survived. And now, all you need is time to rest and to heal."

"You're right." I'd hoped the cards would guide me, but maybe I'm not strong enough for the message they want to give. Not yet. But they're right, the Present for me is the Lovers. There's no escaping that I'm here with Akkan right now. This is something I need to press through to get to whatever awakening is coming with the card of Death. Or hopefully Rebirth. "What does it mean?" I ask Akkan, who's still looking at me with concern. "To mate. What magic does that entail, exactly? Because obviously teleportation is part of the deal."

Akkan rocks back on his heels, but rather than retreating to the couch, he sits cross-legged on the floor before me. "Mating is a fusing of souls. It can only happen if the soul mates are in love. They literally open their hearts to one another, in passionate love-making, and their souls join into one. That releases the magic. The human female expresses her true dragon nature, becoming dragon like her soul mate. He comes into his full powers. They both can teleport. It's... more than that." He pauses to give me that sexy smile. "I only know the stories—and what the mated dragons tell me."

I sigh. My fatigued brain is struggling to put all this together. "You said you've been waiting a long time for me. You were born in 1795. But I was only born forty years ago. That seems like a system that doesn't work very well."

He nods and drops his gaze to the dangling tassel of one of my blankets. "It's never worked very well for me, that's for certain." Then he looks up again. "Your soul was born when I was, Daisy. 1795. My dragon soul broke and half fused with your human one. But of course, I had no idea *which* human girl was my soul mate. For that, we need the witches. When I came of age, sixteen years old, I went to the witch to be paired with my one-and-only soul mate… only to find you had died six years before."

"Wait… I died when I was ten?" A sense of connection fills me.

"Yes, I suppose—"

"Right. I remember that." Everything suddenly fits like pieces of a puzzle falling into place.

"You… *what?*" His eyes go wide, and he leans back.

"I remember my past lives." He's the first person I've told, other than that one past-lives-regression therapist I went to. I thought she would help me work through *why* I could remember. She was more than a little freaked that I already could. "I was out on a boat with my cousins. I don't remember exactly why—I think they were teasing me about learning to fish. Somehow, I fell off the boat and got tangled in the net. Death by drowning is not fun, let me tell you that."

His expression says maybe I shouldn't have shared. "You *remember?*"

"It's not the kind of thing you invent, Akkan." A prickle runs up the back of my neck. The Lovers. *Vulnerability, honesty.* I'm already telling him things I've told no one else. If he's going to make fun of me—

"I believe you," he rushes out. "I just…" He runs his hand across his face, wiping away the shock. "I've never heard of a soul mate who *remembers* her past lives. Always, the slate is wiped clean. If a dragon cannot win her heart the first time they meet, she goes on to live a normal human life. He continues on, unmated. Then, when she is reborn, he has another chance."

I tilt my head to the side. "When you found out I'd died, you waited for another chance with me."

He's wordless for a moment, struggling to say something, but he seems stuck. Finally, he says, "Yes. I waited."

Interesting. Sounds like there's a story there. "In my next life, I was the daughter of a merchant in

Rome. It was a good life, all things considered. Better than being the daughter of a fisherman. There were no dragon soul mates coming to win my heart." I raise an eyebrow. But there's something very *right* about sharing this with him now. As if, *yes*, this is part of my destiny—my purpose. To put these two timelines together, Akkan's and mine. Two souls over two centuries.

Akkan gives me a solemn nod. "That's because I could no longer find you. The Vardigah attacked. Wiped out my entire lair. My mother and father. My brothers. Everyone I knew. They destroyed almost all the witches as well, although I only found that out later. I had no way to find you. Dragons as a species were nearly wiped out that day."

I just blink. *This* I didn't expect. "I'm so sorry." It seems inadequate.

"I didn't think I would ever find you. Do you remember all your lives?"

"Yes." I pause to recall them. "I've had five. Well, six, counting this one. I didn't always remember them, not until after. I think I blocked some of it out. But the last time, I died of a heart attack at sixty-two in 1980, and I distinctly remember thinking, *Well, this isn't bad. I'll get to see the year 2000 for sure."* I smirk. "Wasn't as exciting as I thought it would be."

He's just looking at me with amazement. "Were in you New York then?"

I think back. "No, for that lifetime, I was in Europe. Survived the war—World War II. Before that, I died in the plague, so when I came back the first world war was mostly done. I was in France and Britain, mostly."

"As was I." He's still taking it all in. "And in this lifetime?"

"I was born in the U.S." *I think.* I don't want to dwell on that too much. "I traveled a bit but mainly stayed in New York."

"I've been in the U.S. for decades." He's nodding now. "It's almost as if you were following me. Or perhaps I was following you. I stopped my travels and finally settled in the North Lair up at the Thousand Islands. I was trying to find you again. Before it was too late."

I frown. "Too late?"

"Dragons live a long time, but I'm near the end, Daisy."

My eyebrows lift. He told me that before. "And now you've found me."

"And now I have." He smiles, and it's sweet. Terribly sweet. And sexy too.

And it's all too much, all of a sudden.

My eyelids are pulling down. "You know, for a while there, with the Vardigah, I thought maybe I wouldn't make it. That I'd be on to the next life, whatever that was going to be. I wasn't afraid, not really. But now that I'm sticking around this life-time… well, I'm kind of tired."

"Of course you are." He scrambles up from the floor and takes my hands, easing me gently up out of the chair. Then he holds me around the waist and lets me lean on his arm as he guides me back to the bedrooms.

There are two.

He tucks me into an oversized white-covered bed.

I'm asleep before my head sinks into the pillow.

SIX

Akkan

WHAT I NEED IS SOME *MAGIC*.

The old-school kind with witches and potions and alchemy.

Which is why I'm knocking on the door of a picturesque cottage in the Irish countryside as the sun sinks over the distant sea. I texted ahead. You don't arrive unannounced at the lair of a dragon and his witch-mate. Grace was kind enough to teleport me once Daisy was asleep. I hope I'm not intruding as much as it seems—it's only been a few weeks since these two were mated, and I know that's not the time to come calling.

The witch, Alice, opens the door, but her mate, Constantine, is right behind.

"And here he is!" she proclaims with a grin. "In

the flesh." She's as petite and fiery red-haired as I remember from that day she paired me to Daisy in a different seaside meadow.

Constantine sighs. We've been friends for a couple decades. He's one of the few dragons who survived the fire in Athens, older like me, and is no doubt resenting my presence in their honeymoon.

"I hope I'm not intruding," I rush out.

"Not at all!" Alice grabs hold of my arm and tows me inside. "We've managed a guest or two before, and we'll manage it again." This is clearly directed at Constantine.

The look he gives her in return can be described only as pure adoration. It strikes me because I've only been around a few mated dragons, and they're always painfully obvious in their love, but this is at a different level.

He lifts his eyebrows at me. "You're giving her a chance to match-make. I'd be sure that's what you want."

"Well, um…" I'm not sure how to explain the situation.

He bursts out laughing, shakes his head, drops a kiss on her cheek, and wishes me luck as he trots to the back of the cottage. It's small, but I can see straight through to their bedroom and out into the meadow. Constantine strides out, shifts on his way through the door, and soars into the darkening skies. They must be remote enough that he can fly without fear of discovery.

"Ignore him," Alice says, now pulling me into a small side room that's clearly her apothecary. Or her spell room. It's heavy with wood, from the table laden with cauldrons and boxes and bottles to the bookshelves lined with leather-bound tomes. "He's insatiable that one. Keeps me fierce busy. He'll survive a minute."

"I'm not so sure," I say with a smile. "But I appreciate the help."

"What's your trouble?" She's eager, and it makes the whole thing easier.

"My soul mate, Daisy, was one of the ones captured by the Vardigah."

"I remember." Of course, she does—she paired us.

"She was in a coma for three weeks. Just woke up, but she's still very weak. I recall, from my days as a boy, that witches could use dragon blood to create spells. *Healing spells.* Is that true? And if so, I'm here to offer up as much as you need—for Daisy and any other spell-making you might care to do. I understand our people used to make such exchanges with yours." I give a glance at the books on the shelves and hope the answer lies in there somewhere.

"I like the sound of that." Her green eyes are certainly lit up in the dusty haze of this workshop of hers. "Is she just a bit fatigued? Or is there more to it?"

"Well, there was the torture."

The glee in her eyes at the prospect of magic-making dims a little. "Aye. There was." She purses her lips. "I'm sorry for that, you know. I did what I could."

I dip my head. "You're the only reason I have my mate at all." I know the story—how Alice was tricked into helping the Vardigah find the soul mates and how she was instrumental in getting them free—but I didn't imagine she'd hold so tightly to the guilt.

"Making your love possible… it's what a witch is meant to do." She says it with reverence.

I smile at the sweetness of it then glance again at the books. "Do you have something that will just restore her energy? She's an incredibly strong person. I'm sure, if she were only feeling a little better…" I don't know where I'm going with that. Seducing Daisy is out of the question.

A twinkle returns to Alice's eyes. "I have just the thing." She scurries to the bookshelf and runs her finger along the bindings, scanning them. She quickly finds the one she wants and pulls it down, plopping it heavily on the workbench and flipping through the ornately decorated pages. "Mind you, it'll be some nasty stuff," she muses. "You'll have to convince her to choke it down."

"She's very mystical and seems to take magic for granted." I watch as Alice gathers things from around her workshop. "I don't think it will be a problem." Then I keep quiet as the witch makes her magic, pulling out a somber black pot and tossing things in. Feathery, dusty, herb-like things. And others I'm not sure I could identify. Then she uncorks some wine and pours it over the lot. I take a half step back as she conjures a small blue flame under the pot and stirs with a wooden spoon.

"I'll be needing that dragon blood of yours."

"How much?" I reach for a curved dagger lying on the benchtop.

She sees it and exclaims, "Hold up! Are ye thick?" She gingerly takes it from me, carefully holding the handle. "There's magic on that one. Never mind the rust." She shakes her head, amazed at my recklessness, and carefully stows the blade under her workbench. Then she fishes around a set of tiny drawers until she pulls out a razor blade. She affixes it to an ebony stick and passes the blade end through the blue flame until it heats. "We're doing magic here, not barbarism." She passes the blade-tipped stick. "I'll need a fair bit. Maybe ten drops. Better to make it fifteen. Can ye manage?"

I just slice open my palm and hold it over her pot. It stings, but the problem is more that my dragon healing will seal up the cut before we're done. We wait, counting the steady drip. Then Alice snatches up a tiny blue bottle and holds it to my palm, catching the excess blood and easing us away from the pot.

She holds my hand and the bottle like that, literally bleeding me. "You're doing a fine thing here, Akkan."

"It's nothing." And it truly is. I won't even feel this in a few minutes.

"I mean caring for her." She squeezes my hand to renew the blood flow.

I manage not to wince.

"I know how dragons are," she says. "You love with a fierce passion, and you'd give your life for your mate, but sometimes, you forget that a woman needs something more."

"What's that?" I'm a two-hundred-and-twenty-five-year-old dragon who's loved more women than I can name. Alice looks to be barely eighteen. But she has an aura of real wisdom. And she's *mated*. Which trumps every experience I've ever had.

"She needs a purpose." Alice finishes the blood-letting by sliding the bottle up my palm to capture the last drops then curling my fist closed on the wound. "I saw her, just as you did, in the pairing, Akkan. I got a glimpse of that soul even as she was wrecked. She'll love ye, and she'll need ye, but she's special. You'll have to let her be who she is." She corks the bottle of blood and sets it aside, her payment for her services, then she gives the cauldron a stir. "It's not complicated. But it can be hard." She wrinkles her nose at the smell of the potion. Even from a few feet away, it's like musty bat and boiled wine. She quickly finds another bottle, larger and clear, and decants the potion into it. Corking that, she hands it over. "Now, I will say that's not the worst I've ever drank, but it will be murder to get down. And it'll have an after-kick. Just creeps up on ye and says, *How's it going?*"

"Duly noted." I take the potion. "Thank you, Alice. For the advice as well. I have every intention of letting Daisy be whoever she needs to be. Even if that means without me."

She waves that off. "You'll do grand. Fine, even. Off with you."

I smile and carry out my prize, texting Grace on the way for a ride. She's a chatterbox of questions before she whisks me back to the small island cottage, but then she leaves quickly enough. I peek in on Daisy, but she's sleeping. I leave the potion in the kitchen, and I should sleep as well, but I'm restless. I find myself out on the balcony overlooking the sea. The fresh air, the gentle hills, the soft sound of the port in the evening, warming up with diners, mostly tourists soaking in the beauty of the Isles, all ease my mind a little. I hadn't realized how much I'd missed Greece. After I found the lair burnt to the ground, I didn't return for decades. As I told Daisy, I wandered Europe for a long time. There were many sojourns, some back into temples and caves for contemplation, some through the brothels of each continent in turn. Eventually, I stumbled upon the European lair, but being back among dragons, each fruitlessly romancing one human woman after another, always seeking their one true love... I had no taste for it. It took decades more, a world that modernized around me, and to be honest, nearing my two hundredth birthday before I decided I belonged with dragonkind after all.

At least, at the end of my long and sorry life.

Not that I didn't have love—the human kind, on occasion—but I knew what I was missing all too well. Niko of the North Lair convinced me to try again. To actually romance women once more, but it was a pursuit without spirit. I *knew* my luck wasn't that good—it never had been. Constantine and I spent many nights prowling the streets of the city, but we always knew we were hunting for other men's mates—that we would never find our own.

And then everything changed with Alice. For Constantine most dramatically of all, and I'm truly happy for my friend. But when she paired every dragon on the planet once more, suddenly, there was real hope.

I lean on the balcony wall and gaze at the stars just emerging from the sunset's last fiery herald of the night. Is my luck changing? Or is this simply one more cruel twist the fates have brought me in the end? My soul mate is within reach, after chasing each other's spirits across the centuries, and yet... she has no interest in me. Maybe even an aversion. I've loved enough women to know when one is attracted—and when one is not.

I decide that whatever tomorrow brings, I should be rested for it. I trudge back inside, find my separate bedroom, and turn in for the night.

I awake to the soft, thudding sound of something dragging across the floor. *The kitchen floor,* my mind blearily identifies as it races up to consciousness. *What?* I throw off the covers and race down the hall, through the sitting room, and career into the kitchen only to come to a stumbling stop.

Daisy is eating breakfast.

She startles. "Oh! Good morning." Then she stares. I'm standing, barefoot and disheveled, in just my sleep pants, on the kitchen threshold.

"I thought…" I stall out, not wanting to speak my fears aloud. *That the Vardigah had come for her.* I swallow and try to nonchalantly stride to the second chair of the table. "I'm surprised you're up." I take a seat, feeling slightly ridiculous—I'm half-dressed and still getting my bearings.

"I was hungry." She takes in my bed-head and bare chest, then suddenly looks back to her food. It's only the tiniest hint of attraction—virtually the only I've seen from her—but it raises a ridiculous amount of hope. Not to mention stirs my body in response.

"Is it good?" I reach for a wooden kabob of souvlaki and pull off a bite from one end. She's watching me, so I enjoy the morsel with more obvious relish. "Mmm. Grace found the real thing for us."

She nods and seems flushed. I return the skewer, and she digs into her food again, obviously trying not to meet my gaze or look at my half-naked body. My *need* for her wells up from deep within, everything tightening. I hadn't expected to have to battle lust first thing in the morning, but here we are. Yet, I know it's far too early to even play at this kind of game.

"I have something for you." I get up and retrieve the flask of potion from the countertop. The kitchen is small but exquisite—marble and steel, hanging copper pots and herbs, modern appliances, but an Old World feel. I return to the table and set the clear glass bottle before her.

"What's this?" Her eyes are bright. She seems healthier already, just from the rest.

"It's a potion from the witch who paired us." I wish I could pull back the last part of that, but it's too late. "It's for healing," I add quickly.

She picks up the flask and examines it. "What's in it?" The deep red color of the wine isn't enough to disguise the odd bits and flakes of magic-knows-what floating inside.

"My blood, for one."

"You want me to drink your blood?" Her nose wrinkles, but she uncorks the flask. Then it wrinkles even more.

"That's where the magic comes from." I plead with my eyes. "I know it's awful. Alice said, *It'll be murder to get down.*" I do my best impression of her Irish accent.

It makes Daisy smile, which unexpectedly squeezes my heart. I fiercely beat down all my hopeful expectations. *For the love of magic, Akkan*—a simple smile isn't her falling in love with you.

"I'm already feeling better," she offers, giving the flask a freshly dubious look.

"Did you sleep well?"

"Yeah. And no dreams either." She meets my gaze. "That's a good thing, trust me."

I scoot closer and clasp my hands on the table. "You do look better." The urge to touch her is getting insane.

She smiles again, but it's bashful. "I know I just need to give it time." She swirls the flask and watches the debris dance. "Or maybe some magic dragon blood."

"When I was young, before the Vardigah destroyed everything, dragons and witches did this all the time. We'd pay in blood, which was really nothing—we heal quickly and regenerate our blood even faster. They'd pair us with our soul mates and occasionally make potions such as these. It's an ancient art that Alice is bringing back, almost single-handed."

"It is nice of her to help." But the grimace lingers. "And you." She meets my gaze. "I do appreciate everything you're doing."

"It's nothing. But I *do* desperately want you to try the potion." Which is the truth. "Alice wouldn't have agreed to make it unless it would help. Rest is powerful, but this *is* magic, after all."

She takes a breath. "All right." Then she takes a small taste. "Oh, God!" She almost spits it out.

"I'm sorry." I lay my hand on hers, which is pressed into the tabletop. "I suppose it's more like medicine. I'd take it for you if I could."

"It's okay. I can do this." The grimace is even worse now, but she girds herself and drinks. There's at least a cup of liquid, and she chokes her way through it, nearly gagging at the end. As she finishes the last of it, I jump up and get a glass of water for her. By the time I return, she's gripping the table, looking distinctly sick. "What in the Universe *was* that?"

"I couldn't tell you." I hand her the glass. "And I doubt you'd want to know."

She gulps down the water, but it doesn't seem to help. She curls up over her stomach. "Oh, God... *Akkan.*"

Alarm trips through me. I put my arm around her to keep her from sliding off the chair.

She tries to push me away, but it's for my benefit, not hers. "I'm going to be sick."

"Alice said it would be rough." I stand and then scoop her out of the chair. She fights me then curls up into me, clutching her stomach. "Let's get you to bed." She just moans softly. It rips through me as I hurry her back to her bedroom. I lay her down on the bed, but she's curled up so badly, I slide in behind her and hold her.

She's breathing through her teeth. *"Akkan."* It's plaintive.

"I'm right here." My body is curled up behind hers, my arm cradling her head. I'm stroking her hair, although I'm sure it's more comfort to me than her. She shivers then whimpers so softly, I almost don't hear it. "I'm sorry," I say. What was I think-ing? "I should have waited until you were stronger."

"I'm... *strong.*" She's gritting her teeth and forcing the words through them.

I laugh lightly, even though this is tearing through my heart. "That's what I told Alice. The witch. She knows who you are, of course, because she paired us. She saw you through our connec-tion." I'm babbling on, trying to distract her from the pain. "Of course, she hasn't seen you weather a near-death coma. She doesn't know you brought yourself back from near-extinction at the hands of the Vardigah. She hasn't seen what I've seen. That you're not only beautiful and intelligent and wise, but you have this incredible strength of spirit. It makes sense, with all the lives you've lived. I didn't expect that. It's a gift, Daisy. One I'm so glad I got to see."

She shivers again, strongly, but then her whole body relaxes. She's breathing easier now.

"Doesn't feel like a gift," she says softly, her head resting on my arm.

"Do you feel better?" I pray the worst is already past.

"Yeah. Almost like..." She wiggles and turns over in the bed, now facing me. Her eyes are shining now, even more bright, and there's a flush of red in her cheeks. "I feel it rushing through me." She's gazing at me in wonder, breathless. "It must be that dragon blood of yours. I haven't felt this good in... I don't know how long."

I put a hand to her cheek. "You're hot."

She smirks. "You're not so bad yourself."

We're so close. It takes all my strength not to kiss her. "As in *fever.*" I frown at the dilation of her eyes. Is this part of the potion?

"I thought you said I was beautiful."

"You are, but—"

She suddenly sits up in bed. "I feel so... *good.*" She turns and grips my arm, giving it a good shake. "It *worked,* Akkan!" Then she's off the bed and scurrying around her room before I can say anything. I just watch, amazed, as she yanks off her pajama bottoms. She nearly trips in her haste to get out of those, then paws through the bags I brought back from her friend's apartment. She finds something she likes, pulls it out, drops it on the floor, then lifts her pajama top over her head. She's nearly naked now, just her white panties barely covering her bottom, her breasts loose, nipples tight with the sudden draft they must be feeling. Or maybe the excitement of the potion. She scoops the pile of yellow fabric from the bag off the floor and works it over her head—it's a lightweight dress that takes a bit of work to get on. Once her head emerges, she catches a glimpse of me staring.

She freezes. "Oh. Uh... I didn't mean to—"

"You can undress in front of me anytime." I give her a slow smile. "It's a bit much to ask me to look away."

She scowls at me, but it's delightfully playful as she works her dress the rest of the way down. Her breasts are now cupped with yellow eyelet, the thin straps over her shoulders holding them aloft in a way that makes me want to immediately free them again. The rest is fitted through her waist then flares out, hanging to her knees. It's hemmed with ribbon and nearly see-through, but much more innocent and practical than the white one I'd brought her before.

"Where are my shoes?" She doesn't wait for an answer, just digs through the bags some more, bending over to give me a wonderful view, first of her behind draped in yellow see-through fabric and then her breasts suspended once again.

I sit up and scoot to the edge of the bed. "Can I help?" I want to help her *out* of the dress, but that's a thought that must remain unspoken.

"Got it!" She's found a pair of white sandals. She balances on one leg to put them on, and now I'm flat amazed. Just last night, she needed my help to make it to the bedroom.

"You seem like you're—"

"Let's go!" She's racing out the door of the bedroom before I can blink.

Sweet magic. I bound off the bed after her. "Where are we going?"

"Outside!" she sings. She heads to the balcony just off the sitting room.

"Daisy, wait—"

"Oh, my God, it's *wonderful.*" She's already at the edge of the balcony, throwing her arms wide and tipping her head up to the sun. Her eyes are closed, and she's breathing in the sea air.

I can't help the smile, even though I'm seriously concerned. "Are you okay?"

"No." She takes another deep breath then opens her eyes and whirls to me. "I'm *fantastic.*" Then she takes off again, back into the cottage.

"Daisy, slow down!" I hurry back inside after her.

"Not happening!" she trills as she races through the sitting room and out the front door. Her sandals slap on the stone steps as she takes them, too fast, to the cobblestone street below. I have visions of her tripping and falling and cracking her head on the way down. I dash to catch up to her, and now we're striding along the sidewalk toward the village, the port on one side and the hillside apartments and cottages on the other. There's a small pier up ahead, and she makes a beeline for it. There's no railing or anything, just cleats for the boats to tie up, although it's empty for the moment.

I'm afraid she will barrel right in the drink. *"Daisy!"* I say just as she stops at the very edge.

"Look at this!" She throws her hands out as if to embrace the entire island.

"I know, it's beautiful." I stand close in case I have to pull her back from jumping in.

She grabs my arm and shakes it for emphasis. The mania in her eyes is infectious. "I feel so *good.* God, is this your crazy dragon blood? I feel like I'm high!" She's calming a little, searching my face for answers.

I take her hands in mine. "I guess? It looks good in you." I smile. This moment is perfect, if crazy, hand-in-hand, standing at the edge of the sparkling water in the morning sun, my soul mate so full of life she's bouncing with it.

She closes her eyes as she draws in a deep

breath and lets it out. When her eyes open, they're fixed upon my face. "Thank you. Thank you for this."

"It is entirely my pleasure." I feel the heat of those words. I see it reflected in the darkening of her eyes.

"How would you have found me?" She's a little breathless. We're standing *very* close. "If the witch hadn't paired us. If the Vardigah hadn't taken me. How would you have ever found me?"

I'm not sure if it's a rhetorical question or not. "I've spent the last two decades scouring New York for you." Longer than that, of course, but that's the most recent round, when I actually was *trying*.

"But how did that work? How would you have known it was me?"

I can't resist. I slide one hand to her cheek. "Whenever I found a woman who was vibrant and amazing—dragon spirited in every outward way—I would seduce her into a kiss. A single kiss, if it were a True open-hearted one, would reveal you to me." I'm not pulling her closer, but everything in me wants to.

"Would your soul fuse with hers?" She's not closing the gap, but she's not moving away from my touch, either.

I can't help the heat as I peer into her eyes, searching for her soul there. "No. We'd have to make love for that. We'd have to be *in love* for that, Daisy. A True Kiss is just the first step. The one that reveals what we are." I hear the aching need in my voice.

She must as well because she reaches for me, her hand on my cheek, lifting on her toes, but she barely gets halfway, and I'm already there. My mouth on hers. My fingers sliding into her hair and cradling her head. My tongue slipping into her mouth. Gentle, at first, then the need is too great, and I have to pull her against me. I'm still half-dressed, my chest bare, and her dress is but a whisper between us. I'm already hard, and she has to feel that too, but this kiss is all about cracking open our souls, and *holy magic...* I feel it. The burning sweetness of it. Two hundred years of need crying out through it. Her hands are hot on my skin, clawing at me as I deepen the kiss and weld our bodies together, as close as we can be while not actually mated. It lasts and lasts, each of us grasping at the other until we have to come up for air. We hardly part, still clinging to each other on the pier, putting on a show for any who might be watching from the shops and boats of the port across the water.

"I feel something." She's breathing so heavily, it's nearly a gasp.

I don't think she means the hardness of my body. "That's our soul connection. My soul sees yours. Your soul recognizes mine. It's your dragon finally coming awake, Daisy." My heart is brimming —with hope and fear. Can this really be happening? Will the fates yet snatch it from me?

"Yes." She places her hand flat on my chest. "I feel that too."

I pull back enough to peer in her eyes. "What do you mean... *too?*" If she's talking about our bodies, I'm more than prepared to deliver on the promise mine is making.

"There's something... more." She's frowning at my chest, looking at her hand pressed to it. Then she pulls her hand back to rub against her own chest, right over her heart. "I feel *different.*"

I still think it's the soul connection. Some describe it as an awakening, unlike anything else they've experienced. My soul is rejoicing with it right now. Surely, that's what she means.

But when her gaze draws up to meet mine, she

looks newly astonished. "I finally know who I'm supposed to be."

And the bottom falls out of my world.

Because I'm certain she doesn't mean *a dragon's mate.*

SEVEN

Daisy

EVERYTHING IS GIDDY AND JITTERY.

I have too much energy—I nearly trip on the cobblestones on the street. The rest of the way back to the cottage, Akkan holds my hand to make sure I don't go down.

My body is just reacting to the cascade of things awakening in my heart and soul and mind. It's so confusing, it's no wonder my body doesn't know which way is up. As we hike the stairs back to the cottage, my mind works furiously to settle it out.

My dragon spirit. Akkan said it was awakening, and that kiss—that incredibly hot kiss—definitely cemented that tingly connection we already had. I must have been so bone-weary before that it muted everything. It's hard to feel attraction when your body is simply wiped out. But the potion from Alice has worked a literal miracle—and my libido is singing along with the rest of me. But the kiss didn't just wake up the parts now buzzing and hot for Akkan... it woke up something else.

A memory.

Another life.

One I didn't know I had lived, and if I hadn't spent tortured weeks with the Vardigah, if Akkan hadn't already explained what they were, I might have thought I was dreaming.

Because in this past life, I wasn't human at all.

Akkan pushes open the door to the cottage, his hand still firmly grasping mine, like he thinks I might tumble down the stairs. He brings me inside, but once the door is closed, he wraps his arms around me. It feels incredibly good—*safe*—like this is the one place in the Universe I could finally call home. Which is crazy because we hardly know each other. But as the memories of that prior life come flooding back... maybe that's not entirely true.

He pulls back and holds me by the shoulders. "What do you need? Something to eat? Drink?" His words are sweet, but there's a look of desperation in his eyes. He has to be as confused by all this as I am... but I don't think he understands what's happened.

"I think we need to talk."

He winces but takes my hand once more and leads me to the rattan couch. As we ease down into it, he's still holding my hand, like he's afraid to let go. "Alice said the potion had an after-effect—"

"I'm definitely feeling that." The mania and surge of energy are still running laps through my system.

"It should subside. Maybe this... *different* feeling will go away." He seems to hope it will. But he doesn't understand.

"The kiss triggered a memory, Akkan. Of a past life. One I didn't know I had."

"Oh." His shoulders drop in relief. "You mean before you were my soul mate?"

"Not exactly." I don't know why I'm hesitating. He should believe me. I catch a glimpse of my cards, still out from the reading last night. *Hermit. Lovers. Death/Rebirth.* The Lovers are definitely still in play. Is the Rebirth this new memory? I lean over and pick up the three cards along with the rest of the major arcana. I want to do another reading, but I need to talk this out with Akkan first. I start over-hand shuffling just to ease the jitters in my hands.

"You're going to think this is crazy." I peek up from the shuffle—I have his full attention.

"I doubt it." He's completely serious.

"In this new past life, the one I just remembered…" I bite my lip. "I was kind of the Queen of the Elvish people."

His eyebrows fly up and stay there.

"Not the Vardigah, though. We were called the Dhogerthu—"

"How could you possibly know that?" His eyes are wide. "I… I never told you their name—"

"Because I was their queen." I stop shuffling and hold the cards in my lap. Will Akkan believe me? This feels terribly important.

I wait.

"I… um…" Akkan rubs both hands over his face as if to wipe away the shock. "Okay. You were their *queen?*" He's still wrapping his mind around it.

It's a lot to take in. I'm still piecing it together, to be honest.

"The Dhogerthu live a long time." I squint like I'm trying to see back through time into that other life. "I'd lived for a couple thousand years. It was a peaceful time, mostly. The Vardigah were… *restrained.* That part's a little unclear. I'm still putting together the fragments. But occasionally, the

Vardigah would try some foolishness with the humans—" I laugh a little and lean back, feeling the edges of the Tarot deck. They seem more magical somehow now, almost tingling against my fingertips. "So weird to talk about. But I wasn't *human* then."

Akkan's shaking his head, but I think he believes me. "The Dhogerthu protected us—the dragons, I mean. I guess the humans, too."

I dip my head and waggle my eyebrows. "We had to protect the humans. How else would you mate?"

The amazement squishes up his beautiful face. "How did they—*you*—know so much about us?"

I shrug. That part seems obvious, although I guess I don't really know the answer. "We're all connected. All part of the larger magic of the Universe." This is something I knew even before I had the Elf Queen's memories. "Besides, it was our sacred duty to protect your kind. *My kind.* Our kind." My vocabulary for this is failing me. "What I mean is that we would never let you down."

His amazement drops into a scowl. "But you did."

I draw back. But of course, he's right. "The fire.

The Vardigah attacking. Something must have gone wrong."

"You don't remember?" He's intensely interested in this. As he should be.

I squint again, massaging my temple with the hand not holding the cards. "I remember—" But someone appears behind Akkan.

Vardigah.

I gasp and lurch up from the couch.

The Vardigah roars, and a blast of blue fire erupts from his out-flung hands. I shield my face just as Akkan leaps in front of me, but the fury of it still sends me flying back over the edge of the couch, my cards scattering in the air. A louder growl shakes the room. Suddenly, it's filled with midnight-black dragon. The room is too small for Akkan, but he manages to whirl around, wings battering the walls, blue fire curling over his body. As he attacks the Vardigah, I scramble to my feet and make a run for the door. Just as I reach it, a scream stops me cold. I twist to look, afraid of the worst, but all I see is Akkan's dragon form... and parts of the Vardigah scattered in a quickly growing pool of green blood. Akkan's form shifts human again, gloriously naked and spattered with blood. But there are burn marks across his back, as well.

He whirls to face me. "Are you all right?" he demands as he lurches across the room.

"Yes." I'm gasping for air, adrenaline zinging through my body.

Just before Akkan reaches me, another figure appears between us. We're both taken by surprise. Before Akkan can shift again, another blast of blue fire sends him crashing into the coffee table.

"No!" I scream, lunging to attack the figure from behind before he can blast Akkan again.

He turns—*and he's not Vardigah.* Where their faces are ugly and drawn, this one is slender but with an otherworldly beauty. He has the same pointed ears extending above his head.

"My lady?" he asks, in the Old Tongue. The language of the Dhogerthu. Somehow, I understand him. "Is it truly you, Aerendyl?"

Akkan has shifted behind him, a massive force of black scales writhing against the walls and readying to attack.

"No, wait!" I shout to Akkan, my hands out. I lurch between the two of them, a hand out to each. *"No more!"* I command, my voice rising in power.

Akkan's dragon form freezes. Then he shifts human again. It spears my heart to see the ugly red gashes across his chest where the fire-magic struck him. And behind me…

I turn to face the Dhogerthu. And now that I have a moment to look upon him… "Giullis?"

He gasps—half joy, half relief. "Praise magic, you've truly returned." His gaze is quick, flitting over the scene, assessing with that rare intelligence I've always known him to have. He takes in Akkan's naked form and the dismembered Vardigah behind him. He extends his hand. "My lady, I cannot protect you here. Return to our realm with your mate, and we might have a chance."

I glance at Akkan. "He's not my mate." We're still speaking in Elvish.

Akkan steps closer, chest heaving, horror on his face. "Do you know him?" He obviously hasn't understood us.

"Yes." I reach for him, and he comes to me, clasping my hand. "We need to leave," I tell Akkan. Then to Giullis, in Elvish, "He comes with me."

My faithful servant doesn't even hesitate. He merely takes my hand, and we teleport away.

EIGHT

Akkan

The world of the light elves is unsurprisingly made of light.

Literally everything else astonishes me.

Daisy's speaking in Elvish to the light elf who brought us here. A dozen others have gathered around us, all chattering in the same whispery, tinkling sound of their language. She speaks just like them. If I had any doubts before, they're not only erased—they're obliterated, turned to ash, and buried below the softly-glowing floor. Along with my heart.

Because these are her people. *Obviously.* And I am not, no matter how hard she's gripping my hand, insisting I remain by her side.

The wounds from the battle, seared across my

back and chest, hurt like hell—and will for some time. The one thing that can actually harm a dragon is Elvish fire. But I'll live, which means I'll recover. Eventually. Daisy's yellow dress is charred, but she seems unharmed. *Thank magic.* I managed to take most of the blast. Meanwhile, it's becoming increasingly embarrassing to stand next to her while I'm naked and battered, the light elves fluttering around her with their excitement and surprise. We're in some cramped hall, with seats arranged in a circle around a central altar. I'm fairly certain they want to put her on it and worship her. Doors dot the perimeter of the room, which appears shaped like a star. Every surface glows—floor, ceiling, walls, even the chairs, which look like squishy, oversized marshmallows.

After what seems like an hour, but is probably only minutes, Daisy turns to me. She places her hand flat on my chest and peers up into my eyes, something that would have made my heart soar only half an hour ago, but now just twists the knife in my chest harder.

"You're so hurt." Her gaze is all over my body, but in a concerned way, not a heated one. Her eyes find mine again. "But the Dhogerthu can heal you."

ALISA WOODS

"Did they tell you that?" I can't help the bitterness in my voice.

"Akkan." She grabs hold of my hands and brings them to her chest. "I know this is all so crazy. I can barely understand it myself. But Giullis says we're safe here—"

"Giullis." My voice is cool. "The one who came for you."

"He's my servant." She must hear my jealousy because her face draws down. "Really more of an elite guard—"

"I'm sure." It's petty. I can't help it. This is the fates stealing her away from me again, and I'm quite certain I will not survive it.

"Please just…" She squeezes my hands. "You're hurt. They can heal you. Giullis says they have a healing bath that will—"

"I'll be fine."

"Akkan." She moves closer—close enough to reach up and touch my cheek. "I can't stand seeing you hurt. Please. Go with them." Three Dhogerthu break from the pack and linger around me, expectant.

"You're not coming?" Because of course, she's not.

She pulls away again. "I'm not hurt. And… Giullis wants to talk with me about something."

"Alone."

She gives me a look like I'm being impossibly difficult. And, of course, I am. Because I have a feeling the second she's out of my sight, I will have lost her forever. I pull her close again with our still-joined hands, then cup her cheek with my least-bloodied hand. "I don't know what *Giullis* has to tell you, but there's one thing I don't want you to forget."

"What's that—"

But I'm already kissing her. *Deeply.* I invade her mouth, stake my claim, and let her know with every inch of my naked body pressed against hers that she *belongs* with me. Not *to* me, and she probably was never *only* mine, but she still belongs *with* me. My love for her started the moment we were born, and it will continue until my last breath, whether that's due to Vardigah fire—*or Dhogerthu*—or simply because I'll die of a broken heart when she rejoins her people. It may never have been in those cards of hers for us to be together. The fates may have only needed me to deliver her to *her* destiny—*Arenedyl's destiny*—but that stole none of the heat from our first kiss. It doesn't mean my love is any less blazingly True.

I leave her breathless, which is exactly how it should be.

Then I turn to the waiting Dhogerthu. There are three, all female, and barely dressed. Their bodies would be human except for the unearthly dimensions—a little too tall, a little too thin, their fingers just a bit too long. As if they've been stretched while living in this strange realm, separate from the world and softly glowing with magic. And then there are the ears, of course, pointed and sticking up above their heads.

They lead me out of the star-shaped chamber and down a labyrinth of hallways, also with the same softly-glowing walls. The floor warms my bare feet, and the air is likewise body-temperature— enough that I don't miss my clothes, except for the lack of modesty. Which doesn't seem to trouble them, given their own sheer dresses barely cover their breasts and bottoms. We don't bother speaking, given I don't know their language. Hand gestures and smiles and nods are all that's needed to bring me to a room with a large, circular pool. Light steam hovers over the surface, and a long, sloping ramp leads into it. A pile of sponges lies in a basket at the edge, and they each grab one on the way in.

As the three of them guide me into the water, I'm wondering if the fact that they're female is a coincidence. Their smiles are a little too friendly. The light touches of their hands a little too caress- ing. The water itself is warm and relaxing, with a slight tingle that tells me there's magic as well. Is this a seduction? Are they intending to pry me away from their resurrected queen, so I don't interfere with whatever plans they have for her? As the Elven women soak their sponges and start to wash me, I can easily see this becoming a four-way orgy in the water. My body is already responding to their touches, and whatever magic is in the water is easing away the pain of my wounds.

I've bedded so many women—women *not* my soul mate. I've sequestered myself away in caves and hermitages of my own, waiting for her. And when the waiting was too much, I would emerge and bed every willing female in a hundred-mile radius. But no matter how lovely or kind or sweet— or how madly they fell in love with *me*—they were never the one I was waiting for. Even when I loved them in return, they were never the woman who could complete me. The one who could bear my children. I could never build a family with them which was my own, never have the dragon sons I longed for, never recreate the family I'd lost that day in the fire.

They were only ever *this*—these three women in the pool, lavishing me with their attention, getting a rise out of my body while my heart weeps inside. At least before, I always had the hope that someday before I died—maybe only for a moment—I would find her. In truth, we had that moment. It was on a pier in Greece. It was a passion-filled kiss in a strange Elven realm. And that moment has passed.

The three Elven women stop their ministrations and beckon me to look at my own body. The sear marks are gone. I feel invigorated, physically at least. It appears their healing magic has fulfilled its promise. They lead me from the pool again, and two disappear, teleporting away and leaving one behind. She waves her hand at my body, and a heated wind is stirred all around, drying me quickly. By the time she's finished performing this magic, one of the others has returned with clothing—a toga made of the same sheer fabric as their barely-there dresses. I put it on, but it's hardly concealing anything. I guess I'm their pet now—I probably shouldn't offend them by refusing. They walk me through the labyrinth again, bringing me not back to the star chamber but to a room with an enormous bed. It's draped in sheer fabric all gathered at the top like a circus tent and falling to the sides, but drawn back to reveal the expanse of it. Perhaps now that I'm cleaned up is when the seduction is supposed to occur?

But before I can wonder, they disappear, teleporting away and leaving me alone.

It's all very strange, but so is the mere existence of these people. And Daisy's connection to them. The dragon book of lore, the *Mýthos tou Drákou,* spoke of both the light and dark elves, but no one had seen them in thousands of years. There weren't even descriptions, merely that the two races existed, and the light kept the dark in check, for they had a hatred of dragons, especially mated dragons, due to our venom's ability to kill them. But that was it— almost a mythical tale that could be dismissed as allegory. Until the Vardigah tried to wipe dragonkind out of existence with a simultaneous strike on every lair on the planet.

And here I stand in an Elvish bedroom.

It's beyond fantastical—it's absurd.

The door opens behind me. I turn to see who's planning to seduce me.

It's Daisy. A breath escapes me, and I'm so glad to see her, I forget to be angry or jealous or just plain heartbroken. I cross the room and pull her into an embrace.

She hugs me quickly then pulls back, marveling at my chest. "You're completely healed!"

"I guess the Dhogerthu are good for their word." Then the rest comes rushing back, and I cringe. "What did Giullis have to say?"

She sobers. "Maybe we should sit down for this."

"That good?" My heart's right back to breaking, but I follow her to the bed, where she perches on the side. She's changed clothes as well—her sheer dress is the same fabric as the Dhogerthu women who bathed me, but Daisy's has more adornments. Lace cupped to her breasts, a thin golden belt around her waist, and a high band at her neck which holds up the entire affair. The dress is short in front, baring her knees, but has a long train that's pooled at her feet while she sits.

"I don't know where to start." She grips her knees like she did in the cottage before, and somehow that bit of familiarity loosens the tension in my shoulders.

"You're their resurrected queen," I prompt. "Aerendyl, is it?"

"Yes. And not exactly." She frowns and twists, so she's facing me, tucking her leg up on the bed. "The queen is like… like a Queen Bee. There's only one. When she dies, her spirit passes on, and she is reborn. The new Queen carries the old Queen's memories."

I lean back a little, but this makes some sense— why Daisy would be connected to all this. "It's like a soul mate's spirit—if you're not mated, you keep getting reborn until you find your other half. Only *you* remember your past lives. There's something different about you."

"Yes! Giullis and I had to piece it together—we each only had part of the story."

The mention of her elite guard puts me on edge. "And what did you figure out?" I picture him seducing her with stories of her royal Elven heritage.

"That something went terribly wrong. It's hard to know for sure, but…" She grips my arm and squeezes it. "The dragons are part of this, Akkan. A *key* part."

I lift an eyebrow. "How so?"

She shakes her head like she's frustrated somehow. "Let me start from the beginning. It'll make more sense."

"Okay." But I'm intensely interested now. Because if dragons are part of this, then maybe my part in this drama isn't finished. Maybe there's still a place for me here, with her.

"Normally, the Queen would pick her successor. She would find a suitable human baby—like me—and make a sacred connection with her spirit." Her eyes light up. "It's like when you're paired as a dragon. You're connected across magic space, but you're not *fused* yet."

"Queen Aerendyl picked you."

"Yes! I was nearing the end of the normal two-thousand-year reign. It was time. And my mate was winding down. His final moments were nearing as well."

"Aerendyl had a *mate?*" Did Elves mate like dragons?

Daisy bites her lip. "I'm getting ahead of myself. But it's all tangled up together." Her hand grips her knee again, the one folded up between us on the bed.

"It's okay." I lay my hand on hers. "Take your time."

She sighs. "I wish I had my cards. They've always helped with important decisions."

"What decision do you have to make?" My chest is getting tight.

She pulls her hand away. "It's not just me. It's *you.*"

I lift my eyebrows again. "Me?"

She clasps her hands and presses them to her lips. "I'm doing this all wrong," she mutters.

"Just tell me, Daisy. *Aerendyl.* I'm not even sure what to call you." I'm trying to be patient, but I've been waiting over two hundred years for her—if it will be heartbreak, I just want it done.

"To be honest, I'm not really sure who I am anymore, either." She drops her hands to her lap. "Aerendyl selected me at birth... but she selected *you,* too."

"What?" I have no idea what she means.

"It has always been this way, from one queen to the next. Always the same spirit, every two thousand years, passing down to another dragon-spirited human woman. Normally, there is a great ceremony about it. The Queen knows her time is approaching. She selects a pair at birth—a dragon and his dragon-spirited mate—and she marks them with her spirit. With that blessing, that connection to the magic of the Universe, they grow into adulthood, wise and spiritually inclined beyond their years. Haven't you always felt it, Akkan? The touch of connection to something just a little... *more?*"

All of this is making my heart pound. "Yes. Always. I spent years in retreat, seeking spiritual guidance. I was..." I swallow because this feels too vulnerable. Too open. "I was keeping my soul pure for you." I expect disbelief—she must know I've slept with many women—but she just nods instead.

"If all had gone according to plan, Queen Aerendyl would have approached us once we were paired. Once you'd started your romance of me, but before we'd mated. She would have explained how all of it worked. That if we agreed, and if we mated, that she would begin the ritual, the *Dar-reth.*"

"What's that?" My mind is reeling.

"The sacred transfer. Her soul, her memories, would become mine. Her previous form would pass away, and I would become the new Queen. And you, Akkan, would have been my mate. *The new Queen's Mate.* Because we're two halves of the same dragon soul, right? Queen Arendyl's mate was a dragon, too. And when she passed, his time would end as well. This is the way it has always been, for as long as our kind have lived. We are all connected

—the humans, the Elven, and the dragons. Even the witches have their role in bringing us together. It all works in harmony."

"Until something went wrong." But my heart is soaring with ridiculous hope. Somehow in all of this, I *am* supposed to be with Daisy. *Aerendyl?* I almost don't care how it works. The fates may have a use for me yet… one that actually keeps us together.

"Something went terribly wrong." Daisy sighs. "Giullis never could figure out what happened precisely. One moment, the Queen was receiving guests in her court. The next moment, she dropped dead. The Queen's powers are legendary. She's nearly immortal. There's no poison that could touch her. At first, they thought perhaps she had simply died of natural causes. And of course, her mate had died as well. That was assumed to be because she died. But later, after the confusion and panic settled, Giullis wondered if the Queen's mate had been murdered. Maybe someone—an assassin —somehow reached the Queen's mate and killed *him…* and thus her. Prematurely. Before she could enact the Dar-reth."

"But her soul must have joined with yours anyway." I'm not piecing it together myself.

"Remember how I died when I was ten?" she says. I nod. "I think the problem started there. That reset the clock. Queen Aerendyl had to wait another ten years, just like you, for me to be reborn and to grow to adulthood once again. And she almost made it. But before you and I reached the age of pairing, someone killed her mate. And her. And suddenly, all the Dhogerthu were in chaos. They can't exist in the same way without their queen. She ties them together. It's not just being a leader... there's some actual magic that keeps everything in harmony."

My eyes go wide. "That's when the Vardigah rose up."

She nods solemnly. "The dark forces of the Elven world assembled. Maybe they were the ones who killed the Queen's mate to begin with. Giullis isn't sure. But before he knew what was happening, the Vardigah struck. They went after the dragons—because they knew, Akkan. They knew the Queen might yet still resurrect in a dragon-spirited human woman, and the only way she could come into her powers was by mating with her dragon soul mate. So they sought to destroy all the dragons."

"To keep her from returning." Holy magic. "But she did return. Just now... when we kissed—"

"Just her memories." Daisy peers into my eyes, searching my face for something. "I'm not the Queen, not yet. Giullis says normally, I would mate first, and then the *Dar-reth* would transfer the Queen's memories and powers all at once."

"Wait… so… does that mean—"

"We don't know," she says. "Our kiss awoke her spirit—her memories. But I don't have her powers. I'm not the resurrected Queen. If you and I mated, would that summon forth the rest of her powers? I don't know. There's no precedent for it. There has always been the Dar-reth. Without it… perhaps the Queen's magic is simply gone. And the Vardigah will reign forever."

I just blink, stunned by all this. "This is the choice you have to make," I say to her, "is whether to mate with me and possibly become Queen… or not."

"Yes. And no." She bites her lip again. "Queen Aerendyl would have given us *both* the choice because this affects you too. If you mate with me, it won't be as a dragon, Akkan. You won't come into your dragon powers."

I lean back and frown. "What do you mean?"

"We will both become elves."

NINE

Daisy

IT'S EASY FOR ME TO ACCEPT THE MAGIC.

Maybe because a two-thousand-year-old Elven Queen is living in my head.

The shock on Akkan's face is much more normal. "How can we just *become* elves?" he asks and not without reason.

I shrug. "The Queen has extraordinary powers... I guess? I mean, how can you teleport when you're a mated dragon?"

"It's just part of the deal." But he's frowning now, working it through.

"Right. And we're all connected. The elves watch over the dragons and humans. But their queen is human, originally, and her mate is dragon. So, the elves care for us, but they also depend on us.

Dragons need the witches to pair them with humans for mating, which helps the dragons—and the elves—but the witches need the dragons' blood for their magic. The humans don't have a clue, but they're protected. It's all part of the same magical ecosystem."

He scowls. "How do the Vardigah fit in that ecosystem?"

"They're what happens when things break down." I grab hold of his hand and squeeze. "We can fix this, you and I, Akkan. I mean, we're not sure if it will work. But it will only work if we mate. And, well, I'm not so sure about that."

He looks hurt. "Because you don't want it."

"Do *you?*" I gesture to this ridiculous mating bed that Giullis conjured. "Still? Knowing all this. That it's nothing like you've expected all this time?"

His hurt flies away, replaced by the intensity I've seen on his face so often in the short time I've known him. "I'm an old dragon getting ready to die without his mate. *Nothing* has worked out how I expected."

"But we've just met—"

The back of his fingers stroke across my cheek. "I only needed one kiss to know. All my life, I've heard the stories about how mating was the experience of a lifetime. I believed it. Then I wished it *weren't* true—because I would never find you. And now I have... Daisy..." His blue eyes darken. "If I have to call you *Aerendyl* while I make love to you in an Elvish body... I will. There's nothing that could keep me from mating with you. Nothing except that I don't think you want it."

I frown and take his hand from my cheek and hold it. "My name is Helen."

His eyebrows lift. "Which lifetime was that? The first?"

"No, this one." I drop my gaze to where our hands meet. "Truth is, I don't know my real name. I have all these lives swimming inside me, and I still don't know."

He softens his voice and squeezes my hand. "I don't understand," he says gently.

"I'm afraid..." I sigh, but I should just tell him, no matter how embarrassing. I look up at his concerned expression. "We have to be in love for the mating to work, right? Well..." Before the hurt on his face can settle too deeply, I rush out, "I'm afraid I don't know how to love. Not real love. The kind magic is made of."

His brow scrunches up. "You've lived how many lives and—"

I sigh again. *"Remembering* love isn't the same. I *know* Aerendyl loved her mate. I've had past lives where I loved people, at least for a while. It's like watching a movie, and seeing what it looks like, but that's different than experiencing it for yourself."

"You never found someone?"

I look away, feeling the too-familiar shame that burns along with that question. Because I *should* have been able to do this. Any normal person would. But I'm not normal. I never have been. "I never let anyone get close." My chest feels tight, the shame and pain still as fresh as the day I first found out how *not* normal I was. "I'm pretty sure I'm broken, Akkan."

"Maybe you were just waiting for me." He says it softly, and when I look up again, he's giving me a tentative smile.

I just need to tell him. "I don't know my name because my father lied to me every day of my life."

Akkan's smile fades.

"We were always moving around," I explain, "and I was a child, so what did I know? He took odd jobs. He taught me how to help. My earliest memories are digging through his tool chest to find the right screwdriver. He wasn't a *bad* father—he just wasn't my real one." The frown of confusion on his face says I'm doing a lousy job of this. But it's causing my hands to tremble, so I lock my arms across my chest and keep going. "We moved around a lot. I always thought my mother had died, although he never really said anything about her. Then one day, when I was sixteen, he was hit by a bus on the way to a job. I didn't even know until he didn't come home. It took me three days to find him, searching the hospitals and morgues. When I finally did, he told me—that he wasn't my father. That he'd taken me when I was small. That he *needed* me, someone who belonged just to him. I begged him to tell me who my real family was, but he refused. And then he died." A chill shakes my shoulders. I haven't talked about this in decades.

Akkan's arms are suddenly around me, pulling me into the solid wall of his chest. "Daisy, I'm sorry."

"He told me my real name was Helen," I mumble, my face pressed against the warm comfort of him. "That's all I know." I pull in a deep breath, and the scent of Akkan fills me. Clean from the bath and masculine. I barely know this beautiful man, but I feel the connection between us. That soul bond. It's more than I've ever felt with anyone else… and I'm afraid that's all I'm capable of. I pull back, out of his embrace, and look him in the eye. "He's the only man I've ever loved, and that love was all a lie."

His expression pinches in. *"He* lied, but you loved him like a father. That was real."

I shake my head and look away again. "I was a child. I didn't know any better." I turn back to him, searching his face to see if he can understand this. "I became an adult that day, at sixteen, and I've been on my own ever since. I don't rely on anyone. I take care of myself. And other people too—I keep myself fed and whatever I need by working odd jobs. Like him. It's the one *real* thing he left me, those skills. I use them to help other people. Sometimes for money. Sometimes just to make the world a little better. But I never could trust anyone enough to stick around for very long, you know? And here I am, now, and all I have to do is *love you*, and I can save the world of dragons and elves and humans… and it's the one thing I just don't know how to do."

"What about Grace and Jayda?" There's so much sweetness in his voice.

I hesitate. Do I love them? "They're the closest I've ever had to sisters."

"You took care of each other, right? In the cells.

And after." He peers at me now, tugging my arms, so they unlock from my chest.

"I did readings for them." It's making me choke up, and I don't know why. "Just imaginary ones. I didn't have my cards."

"You were comforting them. Giving them hope." He's stroking the back of my hand.

"I didn't have anything else to give."

"But that's *everything.*" His smile is so gentle. "Love is something you choose to do. If there's one thing I've learned in all my time on this planet, it's that *loving* is a verb. It's an action you decide to take. Maybe your father did it for the wrong reasons. But you did it for Jayda and Grace for the right ones. Don't tell me you're incapable of love. I've already seen it in how they worry about you. How they came to help you. And you'd do the same for them."

"I would." Tears are leaking from my eyes now.

"You already have. Give me a chance, Daisy." His hand is on my cheek. "*Helen.* Aerendyl. Whatever you want me to call you, whoever's memories you have, all I know is the woman before me has a heart that wants to save the world, if only she can figure out how to love. Let's learn together."

"Is it that simple?" My voice is barely a whisper.

He's moving in to kiss me. "I have no idea." Then his lips are on mine, and it's just as hot as the first two times. More because he's leaning me back on the bed, his hand skimming my thigh and already under the diaphanous skirt I was given by Giullis as "more appropriate for a queen." My memories say that's true. They tell me that making love to my mate will be wildly wonderful. But it's Akkan's lips hot against my mouth, my jawline, my neck that convinces me I can take the risk—take the leap—and try.

"This is all I want." His words caress my shoulder. "This is all I've *ever* wanted."

My hands thread into his hair as his lips trail kisses down my chest. He nips at my breast through the dress, then slips his hand inside to free it. The dress is barely clinging to me anyway. I pant and arch up into his teeth grazing my nipple, then he takes it into his mouth. My fingers splay across his back, seeking the hotness of his skin and sliding off the toga that's slung over his shoulder. He lifts off me for a moment to yank the whole thing free. He's truly glorious naked, his erection thick and ready for me. I blink and edge up on my elbows, not entirely sure I'm ready for him. But then he's pressing that well-muscled body against me on the bed, and my body surges heat in response. *It* is definitely ready for this man. My heart is still quivering like a small, frightened bird. He kisses me deeply, his hand under my skirt once more, tugging at my panties. Will we just rush into this? Is that how this will work? I have no idea. Then he breaks the kiss, but only to pull back and use both hands to ease my panties down all the way to my feet.

His eyes are hooded with lust as he skims his body along mine until we're face to face. "What shall I call you?" he whispers as he nuzzles my cheek.

"Your Royal Majesty the Queen will do." I'm breathless. His hand slides between my legs, making me suck in air.

He chuckles, puffing hot air against my skin. "Your Royal Majesty." The heel of his hand presses into my sex. The sudden contact makes me moan. Then he *moves,* his hand making a circular motion that has me squirming. "The *Queen.*" He brings his fingers into the torment, sliding and pressing, then dipping inside me. Memories of the past well up: lovemaking with my mate, the centuries and millennia blurring together, his intimate knowledge of my body giving him free access to my pleasure. Akkan barely knows me, but he's a quick study of the language of my body, knowing just how much pressure brings a gasp, how fast a stroke of his hand elicits an arched back. He's gripping my squirming body, holding me still for his pleasuring. I'm grasping at the bed, his shoulders, the hand between my legs that's racing me to climax. When it comes—*when I come*—the convulsions rock me against him. He holds me fast, whispering his delight at my whimpering, his hand still working every last pulse of pleasure out of me. As it passes, tension flees my body. I sink into the bed, and Akkan relents, at least for the moment, drawing back with glittering eyes and a wicked smile.

"Are all dragons this good at love-making?" My words are slurred with pleasure.

"I'm sure I don't know." But his smirk traces a flush all over my body. Then he reaches for my hands and urges me up until we're kneeling on the bed, facing each other. His hands slide around to the back of my neck, working at the clasps which hold up the entire tangle of my dress. When it drops down, he caresses my breasts on the way down to the thin golden belt at my waist. He holds me close while he works on that, nuzzling me again, his lips brushing kisses along my jawline and neck. In a moment, the belt loosens, and the whole thing slips to my knees. He holds my hands out to the side, admiring my body. I'm no spring chicken anymore, but under Akkan's gaze, my body seems to glow like a goddess. I remember being worshipped like this—Aerendyl's mate would literally place her on an altar and pleasure her again and again. It was an intimate joke between the two of them. This feels like an echo, and yet I've never experienced it first-hand. Never had a man look at me the way Akkan is right now.

Is this love? The feeling of being desired? I don't know, but it's not a terrible thing.

Akkan moves close again and slides his hands along my body like he's trying to touch every last part—caressing my nipples, squeezing my breasts, skimming the small of my back to grasp my rear end. He lifts me up out of the pile of dress and spreads my legs, bringing my sex up against his belly, trapping the hardness of him between us. Then he lays me back on the bed again, and I think maybe this is it—this is when he takes me. But instead, he open-mouth kisses down my body, leaving a trail of wetness that leads to the already-soaked area between my legs. He hikes my knees over his shoulders and lavishes that tongue on me. The jolt is electric this time, and I'm instantly moaning and bucking into him. He wraps his arms under my bottom, lifting me up into his greedy mouth, and I can't help the sounds I'm making now. I paw at the bed, another climax racing up, and when it reaches the peak, my thighs quiver around his head as the rest of me arches and convulses. He draws it out, teasing me further, and before it even abates, his fingers take me, thrusting and compounding the orgasm that's still shaking me. I cry out again, half sitting up and cradling his head in my lap as he renews that orgasm, making it crest again. It keeps rippling through me for an uncountable time. When it finally passes, I collapse back on the bed.

"Is this how you make me love you?" I ask, boneless and breathless. "Multiple, incredible orgasms until I relent?"

He kisses his way back up my body and grins when he reaches my face. "That was just for fun."

"What do you do when you're serious?" My mind is awash in an orgasmic haze.

But his grin does fade, and the heat of that look pulses pleasure through me. "Do you want me serious, my Queen?"

"Call me Daisy. It's the name I picked. The only one that's fully me."

His eyes light up. "Daisy, my love." He kisses me tenderly, and the taste of me is still on his lips. The hardness of his body, all muscles and strength and the thick shaft pressed against my belly, is exciting in its promise. "I want to pleasure you until you can't take it anymore. I want to hear you cry out. I want to reach that peak with you. I want to savor every tiny moment. I don't know if I can win your love in bed, but I'm sure as hell going to try."

That makes me smile. "You're so sure you love me?"

"No question in my mind." He dips his head down to nibble on my shoulder.

I run my fingers through his longish hair. "You're certain you want to be bonded to me. For thousands of years."

He halts mid-kiss, then lifts up to peer into my eyes. "I'd forgotten that part. Oh, hell, never mind."

My mouth opens in shock, but he's already smirking at my surprise.

"You're terrible!" I grab at his shoulders and try to push him away. It's like attempting to move a mountain.

"It's true. I am." He takes my hands and plants them back on the bed on either side of my head, pinning me with his gorgeous body. He slides against me, all hardness and heat. "I want to take you right now, bury myself deep inside you, and pound until you confess your love for me just so I'll allow you to come." I almost think he means it. He lowers himself to lightly kiss my nose. "There's only one problem."

"Only one?" I'm ready to beg him.

"Well, maybe two, but they're connected." He's serious now. "Firstly, no protection. And secondly, you don't love me. Yet."

I know he means that if I don't love him, the mating won't take. "Maybe I will. You know, after the pounding."

A slow smile stretches across his face. "I do have a certain... technique... I can use. All the pounding but no release. Well, none on *my* part." He kisses me again, this time on the lips. "But I'm still worried about the risk, my love. Your body, unless we're mated, can't handle a dragon pregnancy."

It triggers a memory. "Elves," I say, remembering the pain and the joy. I gently hold his cheek. "Our children will be Elven."

A mixed torment crosses his face. He eases back from hovering over me. "I don't understand how that part works."

"Remember how you said we'd learn this

together?" I urge him to roll back on the bed, then climb on top to straddle him. "Let's just try and see what happens."

His eyelids drop to half-mast, and he grips my hips, encouraging me to slide my slick parts along his hard ones. "I think I know what will happen if we do this awhile."

I brace my hands on his chest and grind into him.

He sucks in air between his teeth.

"Can you really keep from coming?" I ask, curious but also enjoying this reversal of positions, me bringing that pleasure to his face.

"It's called *coitus reservatus.*" He groans as I slide along this full length, not taking him in but tormenting him regardless. "It's a form of early birth control—and pleasure enhancement—and I've mastered it, yet now…" He exhales in pleasure as I keep grinding. "I've never made love to my soul mate before. You weaken my control, Daisy."

"Do I?" But I'm enjoying this way too much. I lift up then reach down to position him so I can take him inside. As I do, he groans even louder, gripping my hips harder. I have to take it slow because *holy hotness* he's big, but when I'm seated, I lean forward, breathless. "Can you keep control,

Akkan? Even when I'm the one doing the pounding?"

"How cursed am I that I desperately want to find out?" His voice is strained, and when I rise up and slam back down, he gasps in a way that's utterly satisfying. I do it again just to hear that delicious sound, then I try to find a rhythm, me clinging to his chest and riding him hard while he attempts to breathe through this magic we're making. I'm so focused on tormenting him that my own orgasm rises up, sudden and almost unexpected, taking hold of me and making me shudder and gasp as I struggle to keep pounding down on him. I lose the battle and collapse on him, my body still shaking with the pleasure of it.

He's still stiff within me… and barely breathing hard below me.

I drag my head up to look at him. "Did you enjoy that at all?"

"Oh, yes." His hands slide into my hair. "Especially the part where you came undone around me, my Queen." Then he pulls me in for a deep and sensuous kiss.

It unlocks something inside me. Something pure and good. Like the first time we kissed when it opened up a part of my soul I didn't know existed, this sensual kiss in the midst of our love-making is unlocking a part of my heart I've kept hidden away, protected from a world that seemed full of lies and hidden pain. *I can trust Akkan.* He's laid open his heart, time and again, stood by me while I was injured, giving his own blood to heal me, and now, taking this insane leap into the unknown, willing to transform everything he knows for me.

I can safely give him what I've given no one else. *My heart.*

He finishes the kiss and rolls me over. We're still connected, still intimately twined, but now he's in the position for pounding, and I'm splayed out on the bed at his mercy.

"Are you ready for more, my love?" he asks, a smirk playing across his face.

I touch my fingertips to his lips. He's so beautiful as a man. He was amazing and powerful as a dragon. I wonder what he'll look like in his Elven form.

"I'm ready for all of it," I say.

He frowns and grinds into me. "You already have all of me, Daisy." Then he gives me a tender look. "My heart included."

"And you have mine." My hand cups his cheek. "Make love to me, Akkan."

He closes his eyes briefly, and his lips move in silent prayer. I'm not sure what he's asking from the Universe, but I feel like we already have everything, right here, in this bed.

When he opens his eyes and peers into mine, he says, "You complete me, Daisy. Your soul is my soul. Your heart beats with mine. You are the greatest treasure I will ever have."

"Is that your prayer?" I ask.

"It's my promise." Then he pulls out and strokes in, and it forces any other words from my mind. He quickly picks up the pace, pounding into me and setting my already-electrified nerve endings on fire. He's panting as well, no longer the controlled breathing of before, just raw, passionate energy that's driving into me. He grabs hold of the head-board, angling deeper and gaining more leverage. I'm whimpering and holding onto him, bracing for the orgasm I feel gathering deep inside, quivering me right down to the depths of my soul. It grows in force and strength, then suddenly, shoots up from the depths, a volcanic eruption of pleasure that possesses my body. Akkan growls out some erotic stream of a language I don't understand, and I can feel him hot and hard within me, very much releasing that seed he fought to hold back. But it's okay because I know his words hold true. We are one soul, one heart, bound forever. I feel the heat of it, the elation, as our souls meld as tightly as our bodies, as thoroughly as our hearts. It burns through me, clearing away any doubts that might remain.

I am Daisy and Aerendyl. I am Akkan's soul mate.

The Universe opens in a brand-new way. The magic of it runs through me and fills me. If I had my cards, here in the throes of our climax, with my head thrown back, my eyes closed, and Akkan sunk deep inside me, I wouldn't draw The Lovers. Or even the Empress, although I feel as much a Queen as Aerendyl ever did. No, I would draw the World. Completion and Joy. The end and the beginning. Akkan and I have traveled the world and found our way here—in an otherworldly realm that was always our destination—and the Universe approves.

I revel in the afterglow of our success. Our pleasure. I sink into the bed, eyes still closed, utterly complete. Akkan's breathing hard above me, still deep within me, but I feel his energy spent and his body supine with pleasure. I know we have many more moments like this ahead of us—eons filled with them—but this one is the first.

I open my eyes and am unsurprised to see Akkan transformed.

His eyes are still squeezed tight, pleasure wrenching them shut. I reach up and gently trail my fingers along his ear, starting at the tip. He shudders with pleasure. I'd forgotten the erotic potential of the Elven form. So much for us to explore.

When he finally opens his eyes, he gasps and raises up from where he lay across me. "Daisy. You're… *her.*" He means Aerendyl.

"I'm me," I say with a smile. "And you're still you." I run my fingers up the length of his ear again and watch his eyes fall half-closed as he shudders.

"What is *that?*" Then his gaze sharpens. "Wait, can I…" He works a hand free to caress my ear as well—it goes straight to somewhere in my brain, a whole new pleasure center wrapped up in magic.

"Oh, yes," I breathe, eyes half-closed. "I remember that."

"You need to teach me *all* about this." His heated look is followed by the hardening of him inside me again. That true mixture of dragon stamina and Elven magic is devastating in bed.

I have every intention of teaching Akkan everything I know. In bed and out of it. About the Elven world and how the magic will keep us safe and strong. I have so much to tell him.

But he's already moving, making love to me once again.

The Universe can wait.

TEN

Akkan

HOLY HELL, Daisy's Elven form is hot.

She's on her knees before me, taking half my length into her mouth while working the rest with both hands. That's hot enough, but this position allows me full access to her ears, which I'm working all I can. A sort of massaging stroking motion across the full length, with a small flick at the tip, has her moaning and whimpering even as she tries to pleasure me more.

I think I'm winning.

Her gasp and release of me, suddenly burying her head in my hip and shaking head to toe, tells me I got her there first. Ear-orgasms are fucking amazing, and I just love watching them take Daisy apart. She slumps against me as it passes, her mouth open and gasping against my thigh. But I'm nowhere near done.

I'll never be done with her. Something that almost stupefies me when I think about it. A thousand years. *Two*. We won't be making love *every* second of that, but if I had my way…

I pull Daisy to her feet then quickly bend her over the soft couch we've had brought to our room. We're still in the Elven hideaway that Giullis constructed, all those years ago, to protect the Elves who had remained faithful to the Queen. To await her return with all the hope they could muster. I'm endlessly grateful for his service now, in ways I can't even count.

This couch for one.

It's cushioned, so as I pound into Daisy, it doesn't discomfort her, yet strong enough to hold up to the abuse we've given it. Right now, it braces her hips as I plunge into her from behind. I lean forward and grab hold of those ears—they're sensitive but also tough as hell—and use them as reins to hold Daisy up while I drive into her. She cries out. This is her absolute favorite position— the combination of hard-driving dragon sex and Elven ear-magic makes her wild. She's already screaming out with the pleasure of it, begging me for more.

I give it to her.

I'd give her anything, including the Elven children I know she hopes will form every time my now-Elven seed pumps deep inside her. Which is about to happen because *holy magic* this position is my favorite, too. Daisy screams and quivers and shakes as I ride her, and that tips me over the edge. I groan and slam deep, emptying into her while I stroke the last bits of pleasure from her ear-tips. It lasts a while, and I enjoy every second of it.

When we finally slump together, falling into the soft cushioned embrace of the couch, we're a happy mess of post-orgasm haze and sloppy smiles. We snuggle for a while in our mated bliss. It's everything I've always heard and more—none of my dragon brothers mated with an Elven Queen, after all. I am absolutely smug about that.

"Queen Daisy," I say as I wind a long strand of her hair around my finger. "Should I order up some of that bug juice, or are we heading back to the bed?"

"It's *ambrosia*, and it comes from Universal energy, not bugs." She gives me a look, but I just grin. I'm as Elven as she is now, and that's apparently what we eat, but it'll be a while before I forget what hamburgers taste like. "And we need to clean up," she adds, which puts a serious damper on my fun. "Isn't Niko expecting us soon?"

"He can wait." I move in to kiss her, but she disappears, leaving me alone on the couch.

Damn teleportation. I take a guess and teleport to the bathing room. There she is, gliding into the water, her beautiful body sluicing through and creating a gentle wake behind her. I wade in, hopeful that we're not actually cleaning up, but she shoos away my attempts at an embrace and heads back for the sponges. The pool has magic woven into the water—it would heal us like it did me before—but it also does a fine job of rinsing away all traces of love-making. If that's something that's desired. I do not, in fact, desire it, but apparently, Daisy's ready to move forward with what this means.

You'll have to let her be who she is. Alice's words come back—she was more right than she knew. Or maybe she did. As Daisy says, we're all connected.

I relent and allow Daisy to wash me with actual seriousness and not a prelude to love-making. Once we're both clean, and she swirls up some magic to dry us—I'm a complete neophyte at Elven magic;

that'll take some time to learn—we teleport back to our room. Giullis has stocked the place with all kinds of clothes, and thankfully, Daisy picks out something less revealing than typical Elven attire. It's still gossamer and white, but her dress is regal and somewhat modest with its many layers cascading down her body and dragging along the floor behind her. She remains barefoot, as do I—it's an Elven custom.

I put on the least-revealing thing I can find, essentially a heavier-duty toga than the one I had before.

"You've explained the situation, right?" she checks.

"I've prepared him as best I can." My phone was lost in the initial attack of the Vardigah in the cottage on Hydra, but Giullis went back for it. I explained everything to Niko as best I could via text. Something Giullis also had to ferry back to the real world. No cell service in the Elven realm. "The biggest shock will be simply seeing us."

She nods but doesn't seem concerned. "Ready?"

"More than Niko, I imagine." But I give her a smile.

"Let's stop at the cottage."

I nod, and a moment later, we're there. Giullis

has cleaned up, and he's already brought what few things Daisy wanted—mostly her cards—back to our room. He's busy readying the true royal residence for us, but he's apparently got the entire Elven realm at his disposal now that the Queen has returned. This stop at the cottage is just for me to check messages.

I scroll through a series of questions from Niko as my phone catches up since it was last in cell tower contact. "Nothing that you can't explain in person," I say to Daisy.

"Good. Tell him we'll be right there." She's drifted in her royal Elven dress to the window. The sea is sparkling with the afternoon sun. I couldn't begin to say what day it was without looking at my phone.

"Okay, he's ready for us."

She takes a moment longer, looking out the window, then she turns to me and smiles. My soul mate was gorgeous before our mating, but Elven magic has taken her beauty to new levels. Or perhaps love and my own Elven eyes see her differently now. It doesn't really matter which. But her long-limbed form and pointed ears don't belong in this world anymore—I'm eager for us to return to our realm.

She strides over to take my hand—not strictly necessary for Elven teleportation, but a custom among the light elves, nonetheless—and a moment later, we're standing in Niko's office.

I've known him a long time—only distantly in the Athens lair, given he was still a boy when I left, but more so recently. He's only partially hiding his shock.

He steps away from the desk he's leaning against and extends his hand. "Congratulations are in order, I imagine." He's even more dazzled by Daisy. "To you both." Then he leans back, scouring my Elven features—longer, more slender, and of course, the ears. "Damn."

"I'm sure you have questions," Daisy offers.

"*Yes*. Your majesty?" He scrubs a hand across his face. "Did I get that right?"

She laughs a little then eyes the couch. "May we take a seat?"

"Please." Niko pulls up a chair opposite as we settle in. "I guess the most important thing is the Vardigah. You said in your text that they're no longer a threat, but you hedged on why. Or how. I'm assuming you have them all in custody? I'd like some kind of reassurance before I tell the dragon world their scourge is gone."

"Understandable," Daisy says. "And I can give you that reassurance, but first, you need to understand that the Vardigah and the Dhogerthu are the darkness and the light of the Elven world."

"I can see that much." He gestures to us as if it's obvious.

I exchange a look with Daisy, but it's clear he doesn't really understand. "They're not different species, Niko."

"Well, I can see the resemblance." He tips his head to Daisy. "The light side is *much* better looking."

"The Vardigah are what happens when the darkness within us takes hold," Daisy says.

But Niko's puzzled expression means he'll need it spelled out, just like I did. "Our lore speaks of them as two different races," I explain, "but the reality is more complicated. There is only one Elven race. They are called the Dhogerthu. Being in the light, in brightness and harmony with the Universe, is their natural condition. They're connected to each other and to the human and dragon worlds through the magic that binds us all together. But if something goes wrong, if one of them succumbs to the darkness inside, then it causes a chain reaction of sorts."

"If I'd known," Daisy says, "I could have stopped it. The Queen is the restorative force. The spirit that draws the Dhogerthu toward the light and keeps them working and living and loving together in harmony. But one of the Dhogerthu succumbed to that darker impulse—we're still not sure who or why, but we do know what they did. They killed my mate. And thus me. Or rather Queen Aerendyl."

Niko's shaking his head. "Okay, it's still freaking me out that you have all these memories inside you."

Daisy nods. "It can be a little unsettling. But I have a pretty good idea who I am." She takes my hand and smiles, and that moment is one of those I'll hold in my heart until the end of my days. To Niko, she continues, "When Queen Aerendyl died, it set off a cascade. That one act, because it was so vile, devolved that particular Dhogerthu into what you think of as the Vardigah. It's a shrinking of spirit and magic that shows up on the outside. They appear ugly because they've literally been drained of all the natural goodness inside them. Even their language changes. It's almost incomprehensible to the Dhogerthu still in the light. We know this because we've fought this battle in the past. It's something we always have to guard against. But in my waning years, I guess I missed the signs that this darkness was stirring in the Elven peoples."

"So the Vardigah *are* the Dhogerthu." Niko's brow furrows. "What happens now that you're back?"

"That's the good news," Daisy says, squeezing my hand. "Once the Queen's power was embodied in me—once we were mated—the restorative force rippled through the magic realm where all Dhogerthu and Vardigah are connected. Before that, many Dhogerthu had devolved into Vardigah. That's how they were able to launch an attack on the dragons and nearly destroy you. It's how they were able to capture the other soul mates and torture us. They were after *me*. They didn't know which soul mate I might reside in, so they tried to destroy us all. And they almost succeeded with me."

"But now that you're back, they can't harm you." I turn to Niko. "Or anyone else."

"I still don't understand," he says. "Why not?"

"Because the Vardigah no longer exist," Daisy says, simply. "Once the restorative force was applied, the Vardigah either returned to the light, turning back into Dhogerthu, or they perished. The ones who were too far gone into the darkness were not able to make the transition back to the light. It's unfortunate—I would have rather welcomed them all back into the light—but some simply couldn't bear it."

"I hate to ask, but... do you have some kind of proof?" Niko cringes.

"It's all right. I understand." Daisy rises up from the couch in all her queenly splendor. "You may remember this particular Vardigah." She waves her hand, and suddenly a body appears on the floor of Niko's office.

Vardigah. I rise up quickly from the couch. She didn't tell me this part of the plan. I don't recognize him, but I can tell from Niko's scowl that he does.

"Do you remember him?" she asks Niko.

"Yeah." He looks disgusted. "He's the one who attacked us when we were rescuing Cinder."

"Yes." She makes the body disappear again. "He's also the one who captured Alice and forced her to help them capture the soul mates. He, and several others who participated in the torture, were unable to return to the light. You can assure your dragons and their soul mates that these ones have paid the ultimate price for their crimes."

Niko nods and seems satisfied.

I'm slightly in awe of my mate. She's had only a

couple ten-minute meetings with Giullis to accomplish all this. I know because the rest of the time, she's been in our bed.

"What now for you two?" Niko asks, his smile returning.

"Honeymooning," I say quickly.

Daisy smiles wide. "Yes, honeymooning." She turns back to Niko. "And then you will not see us for at least a thousand years."

"What? Why?" Niko stands a little straighter.

"Because our realm is not yours, and yours is not ours," Daisy says. "Our people are connected, but the balance is better kept when we remain in the worlds to which we belong." She turns to me. "I might want to say goodbye to Grace and Jayda first."

She's asking if I have any goodbyes I want to make.

I take her hand once more. "I have everything I need right here."

Her smile fills my heart with everything I've ever wanted. Love. Home. And eventually... family. With Elven children, we'll have centuries to love and spoil them, more than I ever would have had as a dragon. Daisy and I will have thousands of years to love one another. And when the time comes, I will leave this world with her.

Then the memory of our love will live on in the next Queen.

The fates have finally chosen to smile upon me.

Akkan and Daisy have their HEA, but what really happened when Akkan, as a young dragon, found out his soul mate had already died? And that he had another ten years to await her return? Read his sexy backstory in Akkan (Broken Souls 7).

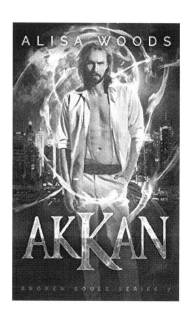

Akkan wants one last night of pleasure before risking his heart with a return home, but a runaway servant girl who saves him from the guards also complicates his plans... and may be just the thing he needs most.

Akkan is a backstory after-novella for the Broken Souls

series. He is the main character in My Dragon Master (Broken Souls 6), and this is his story. Get Akkan (Broken Souls 7) now!

Subscribe to Alisa's newsletter to be the first to find out when her next book releases!

http://smarturl.it/AWsubscribeBARDS

About the Author

Alisa Woods lives in the Midwest with her husband and family, but her heart will always belong to the beaches and mountains where she grew up. She writes sexy paranormal romances about complicated men and the strong women who love them. Her books explore the struggles we all have, where we resist—and succumb to—our most tempting vices as well as our greatest desires. No matter the challenge, Alisa firmly believes that hearts can mend and love will triumph over all.

www.AlisaWoodsAuthor.com

Printed in Poland
by Amazon Fulfillment
Poland Sp. z o.o., Wrocław

58795037R00101